THE RESCUE

THE RESCUE

M R LENNY

LitPrime Solutions
21250 Hawthorne Blvd
Suite 500, Torrance, CA 90503
www.litprime.com
Phone: 1-800-981-9893

Published by LitPrime Solutions: 12/11/2023

ISBN: 979-8-88703-323-5(sc)
ISBN: 979-8-88703-324-2(e)

Library of Congress Control Number: 2023924179

CONTENTS

THE RESCUE

THOMAS WAS LOOKING through his night-vision binoculars watching the convoy of four trucks heading toward him and Willy. Willy was on the opposite side of the road, waiting on the signal from Thomas to fire on the convoy. The trucks were several miles out and closing at a rapid pace. Thomas checked his M60 machine gun to make sure it was loaded and ready; he then picked up his RPG and attached one of the three rockets that he had. He picked up the binoculars, and off in the distance, he could see the trucks approaching. They had to be about a mile away; now the range of the RPG was about four hundred yards. He and Willy were about fifty yards off on both sides of the road, so the trucks will be pretty close by the time they open fire on them. The convoy was close now. Thomas picked up his RPG and aimed at the first truck. "Willy, I will take out the first one, you hit the last one in the convoy. This way we will block them in." "Roger that," he said while preparing his rocket launcher. Thomas knew this was going to be dangerous, but this was going to be one hell of a fight; twelve men and God only knows how many soldiers they might have to face. The intel showed maybe about a hundred or so, but there had to be at least half that many in the trucks heading their way. Plus his team hadn't any success in contacting the helicopters to get them out. This was not looking good, and he was beginning to wonder if this was the right decision to take on this mission. The money was great, "but all money was not good money." He was thinking to himself, what had he gotten himself and his men into? This was not good. This was not good at all.

CHAPTER TWO

Monday
(Kidnapped, the beginning)

MEGAN GREEN WAS the daughter of Peter Green, the billionaire. He made his fortune from oil and real estate. There always seemed to be someone or group that wanted to kidnap him or his daughter, but all attempts had failed. Megan wanted to take a trip to the Middle East to see what life was really like there. She was eighteen and naive about how much danger there was especially for Americans in that part of the world right now. Mr. Green had repeatedly told her no and that she was being a spoiled brat and was just trying to have things her way in spite of what her father or anyone else said. She was stubborn just like her father. Megan was a five-foot-five tall brunette with deep blue eyes and was very shapely. A straight-A student all four years in high school, she played soccer, volleyball, and golf. Megan was offered a full scholarship to Stanford; that is where her father wanted her to go ever since she was a little girl. Before she went to college, she just wanted to experience life on her own this summer; that is why she and three of her friends decided to go to the Middle East to see if what she saw on TV was true. You couldn't always believe what you saw on TV, and her three friends thought the same way—probably just the media overdramatizing the events. So Megan talked James, Karen, and Sandra into going; also, they all had passports and credit cards, so by the time their parents saw the bill, it would be too late to stop them. The reservations were made at a Hilton Hotel in Jordan. From there, they will rent scooters and travel around the city to start their adventure; how excited they were about the trip—no parents or chaperones to tell them want they could or could not do.

James, Karen, and Sandra met at Megan's house on the north side of Dallas. Sandra rang the door bell several times rapidly; this always got under Megan's skin when someone would do that. Once or twice is enough, three or four times just got on her nerves. Megan ran down the stairs quickly to the front door; she opened it to find her three friends standing there, grinning like idiots. "I wish you wouldn't do that," she said annoyingly. "Oh, come on," James said, "are you ready? Do you have your bags packed?"

"Almost done," Megan said, "just have to leave my father a note. Would you be doll and bring down my suitcases, James!" Karen rolled her eyes; Megan could get James to do anything she wanted. James bounced up the stairs with ease to get her bags. "You shouldn't treat him like that, Megan. He is your friend," Karen said. "Oh, come off it, Karen," Sandra said. "Let's get her bags in the car and go. It's time to get this adventure started." By this time James was coming down the stairs with her bags. "Good grief, what do you have in these things, the kitchen sink?" He walked through the front door with a bag in each hand; he threw them in the back of the Chevy Blazer and closed the door. Karen and Sandra climbed in the backseat. James got behind the wheel as they waited for Megan to lock the front door. She ran to the front of the Blazer and jumped in. "Let's go," she said with a big grin. They drove down the driveway and made their way to the highway that would take them to DFW (Dallas/Fort Worth) airport. All the girls were talking and giggling at a very fast pace, James wished they would be quiet just for a few minutes. Man, these girls talk too much, he thought to himself. They arrived at the airport about 3:00 p.m. Their flight didn't leave until 5:25 p.m. James always liked to get to places early. It didn't matter where he was going; he always liked to have just little extra time just in case something came up like traffic or a flat tire. He reached for the ticket at the booth; the gate rose up, and he drove through. James made his way to the garage to park the car; the covered parking was expensive, but it got them close to the gate they were departing from.

They all jumped out, the girls still talking and giggling. Good grief, will they ever shut up, he thought. He opened up the back end of the Blazer and began to pull out the luggage. They made their way to the counter to check in. James, being the gentleman that he was, let the girls go first. Megan was first; each one of her bags was overweight, so was Karen's and Sandra's. They all had to pay the extra fees. James snickered; he put his bags on the scale—forty pounds each. He looked at the girls and smiled; the three of them just looked at him as he walked past them smiling, finally something that would make them shut up.

Walking through security checkpoint, everyone was taking off shoes and belts and emptying their pockets and putting them in the gray tubs once they made it through security. James was sitting on a bench putting his shoes back on, when he noticed Megan talking to a dark-skinned young man that looked like he was from where they were going. She was giggling and talking to him like she knew him for a long time. James walked over to and said, "Megan, let's go. Our gate is this way." He pulled on her arm. Megan hated when boys did that to her. She pulled away. "I can walk on my own, thank you." He let go and looked over his shoulder. The young man was talking on his cell phone in a foreign language. He turned around and kept walking behind the girls. After all, he was the man on this trip; he had to look out for them. He didn't like Megan talking to strange men. Anyway, she always talked too much and tell them things to him they didn't need to know.

They arrived at gate 23, found a spot, and sat down "I am going to get something to eat and drink. Does anyone want anything?" Sandra said. "I will go with you. I'm hungry too," said James. "Bring us something," Karen and Megan said. "Like what?" "It doesn't matter to me," Karen said, "I'm just hungry."

"Same here," Megan chimed in. "Okay," Sandra said, "we will be back in a few minutes." It was about twenty minutes before they came back with burger and fries from McDonald's. James noticed the same young man Megan was talking to by the security area was now at the same gate, and he was talking to Megan again. James walked up to Megan. "Come on, let's eat," he said, not even acknowledging the young man. She turned to James. "That was rude. You shouldn't be telling him your business, my business!"

"Yes, who your father is, where you live, how many kidnap attempts have been made on you and your father. Megan, you give out too much information." When he looked back, the young man was talking on his cell phone again, away from everyone else. I don't like this, he thought. I don't like this at all.

The time seemed to drag before the flight left. They were settling into their seats when James looked up and saw the same young man again. Now he was on the same flight. This is too much, he whispered to himself. Megan sat by the window and was looking out as the young man walked past. James didn't even look at him, and Karen and Sandra were in the seats behind them. They weren't talking too much now. Probably tired, he thought. Well now, maybe he can get some peace and quiet on the flight. The plane rolled down the runway, and then the jet engines roared, and the plane began to take off. James looked at Megan; she turned around and smiled at him. "Well, here we go."

The flight was a long flight even with the showing of a movie and listening to their iPods. They all just wanted to get there and start sightseeing. The plane landed about 6:30 p.m. Everyone was up and awake, trying to look out the plane window to get their first glimpse of Jordan. The four of them got off the plane and made their way to pick up their luggage. Once again, there was Megan talking to the same young man. Will she ever learn, James mumbled to himself. "Megan, let's go!" he shouted. "We have to get a cab and check in at the hotel." She came over, grabbed her luggage, and walked out the door. James looked back at the young man, and he was on his cell phone again. James was getting that nervous feeling you get when you know something was wrong, but you just couldn't quite put your finger on it. He didn't like this feeling.

Once in the cab, they were all looking out the windows, watching the people. Some were shopping, others eating at small cafes, others just walking briskly to some destination. The cab weaved its way down the narrow streets. The cabdriver took a sharp left turn down an alley halfway down; he stopped abruptly and jumped out. James looked back at the girls; they stared back at him in shock. Before they knew it, a black van pulled up behind them, with four armed men with mask covering most of their faces. The first one made his way to the cab and grabbed Sandra from the backseat by her hair. The left side door opened, and Karen was pulled out the same way. Megan grabbed her phone and started texting: "in trouble, in Jordan four armed men"—that was all she was able to type. She hit Send, hoping her father would get the message. One of the men then reached in and grabbed Megan by the arm and yanked hard. She was halfway out of the cab when he grabbed her by the hair, dragging her kicking and screaming back to the van. Another man grabbed James. He tried to fight back; he quickly received a rifle butt to the stomach and then one to the head; everything went black.

Peter Green was on his way to a meeting on the second floor of his office building. He felt his phone vibrate; he pulled it out of his pant pocket and saw that it was Megan. He tapped the screen of his phone to open the message: "in trouble, in Jordan four armed men." Mr. Green dropped his phone; why didn't she listen to him? He bent over, and tears ran down his face; his little girl had been kidnapped.

CHAPTER THREE

Sunday, one week later
(The team)

EVA JAMES WAS the go-between for Thomas's team and the clients; she handled the finances and made sure that the team's money was put into the right investments. With the money they had been making over the years, they all should be well taken care of. Eva was short but with an athletic build; she was trained by Thomas in the martial arts, on weapons, and on how to read people. This she had become very good at over the years. Eva had been trying to contact Thomas but was having a particularly hard time which was unusual for him, so she knew that something was up. She tried one more time on the secure satellite phone that Thomas made sure she had with her at all times. She tried again; this time, he answered. "Where are you!" "What's up," he said. "You didn't answer my question. Where have you been, Thomas?"

"JUST TAKING CARE of some business," he replied. The

reason she was asking was, because there was a lot of money being spent (cash), there had been some big withdrawals out of his account. He had been in the Middle East with some of the men he had worked with over the years. He had been contacted by some of his government connections about Peter Green's daughter, Megan, and some of her friends, who had been kidnapped. Thomas was making preparations for the rescue; he just didn't want her to know that. It would really piss her off, and he just didn't want to hear it. Eva was to be contacted first and set up everything: the cost, the information on the mission, etc. She was to check out the source to make sure that she and the team were not being set up. There were a couple of special ops groups that did not care for Thomas and his team, because they would be contacted if his team didn't want the mission. They felt like they were just as good as Thomas's team, but they weren't. Some of these teams had men killed, had hostages killed, and were sloppy. Thomas's team was precise, never lost a hostage, and never lost a member of his team, plus he had never failed any of their missions. This one was going to prove a little tricky because of the location; it was pretty remote, it was a camp located in the middle of nowhere, and there was only one road that runs through the camp.

He listened to Eva fuss a little while longer; he wasn't really paying attention anyway. She must have realized it when she said, "Thomas, Thomas, are you listening to me? Did you hear what I just said to you?"

"Yea, I will talk to you later."

"No, don't you hang up on me. We have a possible client! Peter Green, the billionaire. His daughter, Megan, has been kidnapped, and he is requesting our services, and he is willing to pay five million per man plus expenses!"

"I will be back in town Monday. Send me the file so I can get the team together. How much time do we have before they decide to go with someone else?"

"Thomas, Mr. Green doesn't want anyone else; he wants your team."

"I will let you know on Tuesday," he said as he hung up his

satellite phone. He was already in the airport getting ready to board his plane when she called. He was tired from all the preparations he had already made—a place he called "The Alamo" (his last line of defense). He just felt a little uneasy about this one and was trying to take every precaution to make sure they could get out once he had the hostages. There were a few men he left there to watch over everything, ones he knows he can trust and depend on. He sat down in his seat to get settled; this was going to be a long flight, and he had planned on sleeping for most of it.

The plane landed, and he made his way to the luggage claim area. He retrieved his bags and walked out to the double doors to catch the courtesy bus to his car. His car was a 1980 Trans Am, the Burt Reynolds edition. Instead of black, his was painted blue, had chrome wheels, and had custom tan leather bucket seats. This was his baby; he had a GMC SUV also, but he preferred to drive the Trans Am; he put in a CD, Johnny "Guitar" Watson. Thomas only played old-school music or jazz in his car. This music of today doesn't have a thing to say, he thought. As the CD began to play, a big smile came across his face. It was about 7:45 p.m., the sun was starting to set. He had the T-tops off. I could just drive for hours, he thought to himself. He made his way to the exit booth. "That will be one hundred and thirty-six dollars," the booth attendant said. He pulled out a roll of cash, peeled off a hundred-dollar bill and a fifty, and handed it to the attendant. "Fourteen dollars is your change," she said. "Have a good evening." He then proceeded to go home and relax for the rest of the evening, but first he needed to make some calls; first was Willy Johnson, tall, light-skinned black man. He was an expert in the martial arts and weapons and was a pilot also; if it had wings, more than likely Willy could fly it.

Willy looked at his phone to check the number; he realized it was Thomas and answered, "What's up, Thomas?"

"Hey, we need to meet."

"Where and when," Willy said.

"At your place. Secure one of your airplane hangars for Tuesday at 8:00 a.m."

"All right, see you then." Willy never even questioned Thomas; he knew when he called it was a mission, and it always paid well. That was how he was able to get this private airstrip here in Arlington started, and he had done very well for himself. Next on the list was Lyle Smith, a stocky but well-built dark-skinned black man who always looked mean. Lyle was an expert in explosives and weapons. Thomas dialed his number. Lyle picked up the phone; he could hear the Johnny "Guitar" Watson CD playing in the background, and he knew right away that it was Thomas. "Thomas," he said, "I know this is you." Thomas laughed for a second and said, "Yea, it's me. Look, we need to meet Tuesday at Willy's at 8:00 a.m., can you make?" Lyle said, "Wouldn't miss it. Do we have a mission?"

"Yes, we do. I will explain everything tomorrow. See you there." Now let's call that crazy Oscar Flores. Oscar was Mexican, about average height and build, but was one mean dude when it came to fighting. He was not afraid of anyone or anything. Oscar was also an expert in the martial arts and computers and was a good pilot and mechanic. Oscar was working on his laptop when he received the call from Thomas. "Oscar, I'm getting the team together tomorrow at 8:00 a.m. Can you make it? I really need you to be there!" Oscar didn't say anything at first; he was still busy looking at his laptop. "Oscar, did you hear me!"

"Yea, yea, where are we meeting?"

"Willy's place at 8:00 a.m. tomorrow."

"I will be there."

"Good. See you tomorrow."

Thomas called Steve Smits next. Steve was the youngest of Thomas's team. He was about five foot nine and about a hundred seventy-five pounds, and he was a crazy white guy who could make use of anything handy and would do just about anything. Steve was jack-of-all-trades; he could do anything which made him quite handy to have on the team. Now Thomas had to call in a few other men that he and his team had worked with before, people he knew he could trust and depend on. All of Thomas's team were ex-black ops agents; the other men were ex-Navy Seals or Delta, all highly skilled.

CHAPTER FOUR

THE VAN BOUNCED down the unpaved road. Meagan and her friends were blindfolded and their hands tied behind their backs. They couldn't sit up with the van taking sharp turns and bouncing around. Megan could smell the musk of the kidnappers; she didn't know what the van was used for before but it had a strong stench that made her nauseous. She strained her eyes, trying to get a glimpse of something, anything that would give her an idea of where they were going or what these men looked like. The van had no windows in the back where they were, and the blindfold was made of dark cloth which made it almost impossible for her to see anything. They had been traveling for hours when the van came to a sudden stop; they slid forward from the van stopping so quickly. James could hear a lot of commotion outside the van. He couldn't make out what was being said. The doors of the van opened, and once again, they were snatched out roughly and thrown up against a wall. Sandra hit her head, as she was thrown like a rag doll. The pain was sharp, and she could feel blood running down her face. She shrieked in pain and could hardly keep her feet. Karen was next to her and could hear what sounded like a rusty door opening and the bad odor that came from inside.

They were shoved in to separate cells; Megan and James in one and Sandra and Karen in another. The kidnappers took off their blindfolds and untied their hands. It was dark and damp. Sandra and Karen started to cry. One of the kidnappers told her in broken English to shut up and slapped them both hard, knocking them down face-first against the cell floor. James and Megan held each other. "Leave them," she shouted, "you don't have to do that." The kidnapper turned his attention from Sandra and Karen to James and Megan. He quickly walked over to them and grabbed them both by the throat; his teeth were bad and his breath was even worse. He squeezed their throats to the point where they almost passed out. He then shoved them back against the cell wall; they both were coughing and gasping for air as they fell to the floor.

The doors were then slammed shut; two men were in this part of the building, one at each end of the hallway, standing guard armed with AK-47s. all four of the kids were just sitting there, wondering what would become of them, how long would they be here. This is not at all what they had in mind for adventure in the Middle East.

CHAPTER FIVE

T WAS 6:30 a.m. Tuesday as Thomas was leaving his house in Mansfield for the meeting at Willy's, the morning was cool. He left his Envoy in the garage and hopped into his Trans Am, he turned the key, and the engine roared to life. He reached into the glove compartment, pulled out another old-school CD. Lakeside, this was one of his favorite CDs; he slipped the disk in the stereo; music blared from his Bose stereo system as he pulled out of his driveway and drove down the street. He was sure he woke up some of the neighbors as he left his neighborhood. It only took about fifteen minutes to get to Willy's place; when he pulled in, he could see several cars and trucks already parked outside of the hangar. Thomas got out of his car and stretched, picked up his laptop and projector, and walked inside. Everyone was there; he greeted them saying, "Good morning, gentlemen, I hope you all had a good night sleep." He said, as he was setting up the projector, "We have an assignment that has to be done in two days starting Friday night, so pay close attention." As he started the presentation, the first several slides were of Peter Green and his daughter, Megan, and her friends. The rest were of the terrain the camp where the hostages were being held. "This will be a night extraction; we will be doing a HALO drop from 30,000 feet.

I have some men already on the ground here." He pointed to a spot on the slide with a laser pointer. "There has been some preparations already made; we will make the rest when we get there.

"There about a hundred men in the camp; most are at the east end of the town. There are eight men guarding the hostages in this building on the opposite end of the camp; here we have to be quick and quiet. Now, Willy, I will need you here about a hundred yards outside the camp covering our exit; we will pick you up on our way out."

"What do you want me to use to cover you with?"

"A 50-caliber sniper rifle with about thirty rounds should do the trick. I will need four others with me to enter the building where the hostages are. Lyle, you will cover the street, Oscar will enter the rear of the building, and me and Steve will go in the front."

"How will we get them out after we rescue them?" one of the men asked. "Well, it looks like they keep several trucks by the building for some reason; we will have to take one of them to use for our escape.

"Now I will have three men at the east end of the camp planting a few land mines on the road that leads from the main camp here, where there are at least four hundred soldiers and three tanks. This will slow them down just in case things start to get a little crazy and they decide to come and help. Now these three men also will have to set a few explosive charges here where they keep a fuel truck and some light armored vehicles. Why do we need this if we are to get in and out quietly! This is for, let's just say, for a contingency plan just in case things go wrong; we can't plan for everything, but we can have a plan B. Gentlemen, this will be no walk in the park; once they discover the hostages are gone, they will come looking for them and the people who helped them escape. Once we leave the camp, we will pick up Willy here and then proceed west for about two miles, Willy and I will get out and set up an ambush here."

"What will we be armed with?" Willy asked.

"We will have RPGs with three rounds each and M60 machine guns with about five hundred rounds. Willy, we will booby trap the M60s after we are finished; they will more than likely try to use them if they can, so we can't let them have those. Then we will have to hump it for about a mile to catch up with the truck. We will then proceed to what I call the Alamo, this is rock formation with a sixty-foot face, a large opening and room enough to house us for a couple of days if need be. It gives us a good vantage point, and we can see for miles, in case they try to send more troops after us.

"This area, we will be able to defend it better than any other spot I found. What we will have to do is set up a kill zone. We have to make them funnel into a smaller area so we can concentrate our firepower on them."

"Thomas, what will be used here to defend ourselves?" Oscar Flores asked. "I mean, Thomas, they will come at us hard and heavy."

"I know," Thomas said, "that's why there will be three Vulcan M134 miniguns with about 6,000 rounds for each gun. There will also be two snipers with 50-caliber rifles with thirty rounds each; they will be placed one on each side. We will also have at our disposal five M252 81mm mortar range of 5,700 meters (three and half miles) with fifty NSB rounds (near surface burst) for each mortar. We will also have a minefield hundred yards long and three hundred yards wide; beyond that, we will first have another ambush. I'm sure after the first one, they will send more men on the second attack along with tanks, so we will set up here about two miles from the Alamo. What we will do is have several two-man teams one here and one on the other side here. Now each team will be armed with RPGs with five rounds each; as you fall back, you will be covered by two 50-cals here spaced about thirty yards apart. The last stand will be the Alamo where we will have devastating kill zone waiting for them. We should be out of here; by then, the helicopters should pick us here on the back side of the rock formation, any questions? Yes." Steve said, "Worst-case scenario."

"Well, if we get overran," Thomas said, "we will have to make a run for it; so I hope you guys are in good shape. It is about fifteen miles to the airstrip where the plane will be waiting to take us and the hostage out of there.

"One last question."

"What is it, Lyle?"

"How much for this one?"

"This mission five million dollars," Thomas said, as he was breaking down the projector and his laptop. "Five million for all of us? That's not very much, Thomas, you know we have been paid a lot more for our other jobs." Thomas stopped what he was doing and looked at all of them. "I'm sorry. That is five million per man plus expenses!" Everyone was quiet for a few seconds. "That's right, fellas. This could be our last job; we are all getting a little old for this kind of work, and I figured we might as well go out rich. So with that being said, get your gear together and meet me here Friday, because we need to leave early around 3:00 p.m." All of the men filed out of the hangar, excited about the mission. Thomas put the laptop and the projector in the backseat then got in his car and sped off; he felt a little uneasy. Something was wrong, he had this feeling before, and he just couldn't shake it.

CHAPTER SIX

Ambush

PRESIDENT WILKINS LANDED earlier at an undisclosed location in the Middle East for his meetings with top leaders in the area, while he was supposed to be at Camp David on vacation. Against his advisor's advice and concerns on the trouble that the region was in make not safe for him to go, the president felt this meeting had to take place in order to try to restore peace and to get the hostages released. The trip to the meeting place was uneventful, and the convoy made it to destination safely. The president was greeted by the leaders and they proceeded into the meeting room. During the meeting, there were some heated discussions; the biggest problem arose when he started talking about the release of the hostages. Most of the leaders felt like he was accusing them all that they had something to do with the kidnapping; this started to make them irate, and the meeting was taking a turn for the worse and was not going as he had hoped.

President Wilkins decided to close the meeting with an apology and said that he was not accusing them of kidnapping; it's just that if any of them had any knowledge of where the kids where, he would be so grateful if they would help in anyway. The president and his bodyguards exited the building and made their way to the five vehicles parked in front. President Wilkins entered the middle SUV along with four agents; he had twenty guards, all armed with AR-15 Beowulf (a modified AR-15 that uses 50-caliber rounds). The convoy started down the narrow dirt road that led out of the small isolated town. All the agents had the same thing in mind they; did not like this location, too easy for something to happen. One of the agents had an American newspaper in his possession. President Wilkins noticed this and asks the agent if he could read it, because they had about a forty-five-minute drive back to the airstrip where his plane was waiting. The dirt road was winding and very narrow; at certain points, his guards' heads were on a swivel. This was not the safest road; anywhere along this road, they could be ambushed, and it would be a while before anyone would know or be able to help if that were to happen. It was hard to see the vehicle in front or behind the president's with all the dust that was being kicked up by the convoy.

The convoy was about twenty minutes way from the airstrip when what they feared was about to happen; the convoy was passing through a part of the road where it widened with huge boulders on both sides. That's when it happened; the first SUVs of the convoy burst into flames, then it tilted and rolled over from the force of the explosion and slid on its side for about twenty feet and blocked the road. Every vehicle in the convoy slammed on brakes and started to go in reverse, "GO! GO!" is all that was said over their earpieces and radios. No sooner than they started to go back, the last SUV in convoy burst into flames; the vehicle behind the president's tried to ram it to clear the way, but it got hung up on the flaming SUV. Everybody out now! The three SUVs stopped, and they jumped out quickly. The agents with President Wilkins pushed him to the ground to keep him out of harm's way. They got into defensive positions; bullets were riddling the SUVs. The guards returned fire. Agent

Adams, who was covering the president, was calling in the ambush. With all the noise from the gunfire and explosions, he couldn't tell whether his message got through or not. Agent Adams looked up to see the SUV in front of his explode; it knocked the four agents off their feet. They all landed like ragdolls, their legs and arms were twisted in ways that he knew was abnormal. He told the president to stay down, as he looked for a place they could use for cover; staying here was not good. He signaled to the men in the vehicle behind his to make a run for a big pile of rocks that's was about ten yards away. The agents acknowledged his signal with a nod. Agent Adams and the other agents that were in his vehicle started to lay down cover fire. Some of the bandits were ripped to pieces by the 50-caliber rounds ripping through their bodies; they managed to kill three of them. The other agents ran toward the pile of rocks. They were almost there when they were gunned downed; they didn't have a chance. Agent Adams took a deep breath, he put in another thirty-round clip; he pushed the president under the SUV. It was evident they wouldn't hit this one with an RPG in fear of hitting the president; they wanted him alive! The bandits started coming in closer; the agents lie down on their stomachs to make smaller targets for the them to shoot at. The agents laid down a ferocious volley of gunfire at the armed men. They took out six before the agent that was by the front of SUV was hit while trying to reload. Then the one behind him was hit also. Now there was only two of them left to protect the president. Adams didn't know what made him look up. The door of the SUV was opened about twelve inches, and he could see two grenades. He grabbed them and dropped back down on his stomach. He could see the feet of the bandits coming their way. He pulled the pin and tossed one their way; the grenade exploded. There was a flash of red, as the explosion took off legs and feet. The other agent with Adams got up on his knees and fired his AR-15 on full auto at the oncoming armed men, taking out three more before he was hit multiple times; his body fell to the ground in a heap.

Adams took the last grenade and tossed it toward the front of the SUV. It exploded in midair. About four feet from the ground, the effects were devastating. It took out four more, but it was not enough. He turned just in time to see some of them coming from behind the back of the SUV. He spun around, fired taking out two more before he was shot in the leg. The pain was excruciating, as he grabbed it with his right hand; he fell and managed to spin around to empty his clip in another one. It ripped his body to shreds; it was horrible sight even if he deserved it. The damage the 50-cal rounds did to this man's body was horrific to say the least. He tried to use his rifle as a club to fight them off but to no avail. He caught a rifle butt to the head, everything went black, as he landed face-first in the dirt. The armed bandits raised and fired their rifles in the air and started yelling. The president was dragged from underneath the SUV violently and was blindfolded and his hands tied behind his back. They picked him up and pushed and pulled him until he was tossed in the van. They picked up Agent Adams, threw him in the van next to the president.

CHAPTER SEVEN

IT WAS AROUND eight o'clock and the evening was warm with a warm breeze, Eva was at her office on the south side of town. It was a property that she and Thomas had purchased together. It was a two-story brick building that needed some more repair before they could rent it out. Eva's office was on the second floor. It faced toward the elevators and set of stairs that lead down to the main lobby of the building. She preferred her desk facing this way, because she could see who was coming. There was a window behind her desk; she looked out. It was getting dark. She turned on the lights in her office, the ones in the hallway were already on. Some of the bulbs had to be replaced, so the lighting was kind of dim. She saw a dark-colored sedan that had circled the block several times. She shrugged her shoulders and thought they were probably lost. About five minutes later, she looked upped from her laptop to see a tall, slender white man coming toward her office. She slipped her Sig Sauer 9mm handgun from her computer bag. Thomas had always told her to keep it with her at all times due to the nature of their business. She pulled back the slide to put one round in the chamber. Thomas had told her that you could never be too careful. As the man came closer, she noticed several things about him. He had a slim but athletic build. While he was walking toward her office, she could tell that he was checking things out. *What does he want, and more important, how did he get in the building,* she thought to herself, as he came closer. Eva kept one hand on the Sig and the other on the keyboard of her laptop. He entered the office and introduced himself as John Hunter. They exchanged pleasantries. "Well, John Hunter, who are you with and what can I do for you?"

"I AM WITH, let's say, an interested party who wants your friend Thomas to stand down on this mission."

"STAND DOWN! WHAT do you mean by that?"

"WELL, HE NEEDS to turn down this mission and let someone else handle it!" he said, as he sat back in his chair.

"I WISH I could help you, but I can't for one, what are you talking about?"

"OH, MISS JAMES, must we play games. You call him and tell him that the mission has been canceled."

Eva looked at him, and she gripped her hand tighter on the pistol in her right hand. "Well, John, is it?"

"Yes!" he said, with a slight smirk on his face, "it would be in your best interest to make that call now, before things get, let's say, unpleasant."

The hairs on the back of her neck stood up when he said that; it was trouble, big trouble, she thought, and at that time, he reached into his jacket. It seemed like it was happening in slow motion. Eva saw the handgun coming from underneath his jacket. With one quick motion, she raised the gun and fired twice, one catching him in the forehead. His head jerked backed as the second round caught him right below his left eye, knocking him out of the chair. She sat there stunned for a few seconds, still holding the gun pointed at where he once was sitting. She didn't have time to even think before she noticed more figures at the top of the stairs coming her way. Eva fired, emptying the clip; she quickly popped in another clip and slid down behind her desk and grabbed her cell phone and hit speed dial.

Thomas was out getting something to eat—angel hair pasta and meatballs, one of his favorite meals. As he was getting into his car, his cell phone began to ring. "This is Thomas!" "Thomas, Thomas," a frantic voice said. "Eva, what's wrong?" He heard gunshots. "Where are you!"

"At my office, hurry please!" He started the car and sped off, the tires screeching and white smoke bellowed from behind his Trans Am as the car accelerated to sixty miles per hour in just a few seconds; he wasn't that far away, maybe ten minutes.

Eva was still behind her desk; she had emptied another clip and had only one left, and she could see that one of the figures was at the doorway to her office. When she heard a blink, it was the sound of glass breaking from the window that was right above her now. The man's head snapped back, and he fell like a sack of potatoes; another one tried to enter the office, and his fate was the same. What the hell, what the hell! she thought to herself. Two more tried to rush the door at the same time. One caught a bullet right in the forehead, about the same place she had shot the guy who was sitting in her office. The next guy was shot in the left side of his chest. It probably hit his heart; he stood there for a second and then fell face-first on the floor. The last guy tried to rush the door at full speed only to get hit three times center mass. All three rounds were close together, maybe an inch apart; whoever was doing this was one hell of a shot.

She peeked around the corner of her desk. She couldn't see any more of them; nothing was moving. Was that all of them? Eva waited for a minute and sat back and leaned against the wall; she was still behind her desk. She heard footsteps; she leaned over to get a glimpse. It was Thomas. She put her head between her knees and said "thank God" when he got to the door of her office. The five men were piled on top of each other, and he could see one in the office lying on his side with the back side of his head blown away. "Eva, are you okay? Eva, are you in here?"

"Yes!" He could hear her say. "I'm okay. How did you, how could you get here in time to do this?"

"This wasn't me" He looked out the window in her office, and she saw him tap his chest three times. He helped her to her feet. "Are you hurt?"

"No, I'm okay, just a little shaken up."

"Good. Get your stuff and let's get out of here."

She started putting her things in her bag, and she grabbed her laptop, when she looked up and saw Thomas talking to someone. Now what, she thought! She walked over to where the two were talking. She looked back to make sure she didn't forget anything. When she turned back around, it was just Thomas standing there. "Who in the hell was that Thomas?"

"Let's go," he said.

"But what about this, this situation!"

"It will be taken care of, for now let's get you out of here."

"What's going on? Why would those men try to kill me?" All he said was "you better stay with me tonight; we will come back in the morning."

"This was strange, surely someone heard the shots! Why aren't the police here; why aren't there any sirens!"

Everyone was going about their business as they left the office parking lot. It was about twenty minutes to Thomas's house; she followed close behind him all the way there. As they approached his house, the garage door opened; he signaled for her to pull in. He jumped out of his car and closed the garage door. "You can have the spare room at the end of the hall, and there are clean towels in the hall closet," he said. Eva went down the hallway, clutching her laptop to her chest. Neither one said a word, she sat on the edge of the bed, thinking what the hell just happened and who was that mysterious figure Thomas was talking to. She went down the hall to take her shower; the hot water felt good, and it seemed to relax her which was just what she needed. She dried off and put on the robe that was hanging on the back of the bathroom door. It was way too big for her; it had to be Thomas's. She went back to her room and went through the dresser and found a big T-shirt, slipped it on, and got underneath the covers. She lay there for a minute, and it came to her who that was Thomas was talking to back at her office. There are two men she had never met and none of the other members had either. Thomas just referred to them as "The Ghosts." All she knew was that one of them just saved her life, and she was truly thankful; she turned over and fell quickly asleep. She felt safe at Thomas's house; he wouldn't let anything happen to her, this she was sure of.

CHAPTER EIGHT

THE DIRECTOR OF the Secret Service, Roy Stiller, was awakened by the phone on his bedside nightstand; it took him a few seconds to collect himself before he answered. "Hello," he said. The voice on the phone said that President Wilkins's convoy has been attacked, and he has been kidnapped. He sat up and said, "Say again!"

"MR. DIRECTOR, I say again the president's convoy has been attacked and he has been kidnapped! Get the contact list get everyone together in the conference room now! I will call the chief of staff myself." He hung up the phone. Great, just great, he mumbled to himself, as he got dressed. He dashed out of his room and out of his house as fast as his legs could carry him, jumped in his car and sped off.

When the director, Stiller, reached the conference room, everyone had assembled; conversations were fast and furious on what should be done. Chief of staff Miller saw the director come in; their eyes met. There was no love lost between these two. The director took his seat. "Okay, gentlemen, tell me what you know." Miller stood up. "We got this distress call fifteen minutes ago, listen to this: 'This is Agent Adams. The president's convoy is under attack. I repeat. the president's convoy is under attack.'" They heard gunfire, then an explosion, then silence. "We have a Seal team that is on the way, we need to do this quickly and quietly as possible, and how soon before they get there?" Miller stated. "We should be hearing from them soon." No sooner than he said that, they received a call the Seal team had been ambushed, one KIA (killed in action), three wounded, and they had to pull back. The room was silent, as they all leaned back in their chairs. "What now?" Miller said. Director Stiller stood up slowly. "We have an option; there is a team that will be on the ground in about twenty hours."

"What team!" Miller said sarcastically.

"The Guardians! The Guardians!"

"Thomas Well's men?" the chief said.

"Yes, that is correct. They are going in to get Peter Green's daughter; as we all know, he has done missions for us before, and he and his team have not failed us yet.

"So while he is there, why not have him rescue the president."

"Wait a minute," one of the other men at the table said, "how is he going to do this? To coordinate something like this in such a short notice is crazy. We need to plan an extraction point, we need to know where the president is being held, how many men will be needed, and how many of the bandits, kidnappers, or soldiers or whatever group is responsible, how many are there?"

"Call it a stroke of luck a coincidence or whatever, it seems where the president was kidnapped is close to where Peter Green's daughter and her friends are being held; from what we know now, he will be probably held there for a short period of time, so we need to act fast. Can you contact him?"

"Already done, I called my contact on the way here, and the wheels are already in motion."

"Do you really the think this will work?" Chief Miller said. "Thomas has never let us down, and knowing him like I do, he will do this and get Mr. Green's daughter at the same time. He will get everyone out or die trying, this I can assure you."

CHAPTER NINE

PRESIDENT WILKINS AND Agent Adams bounced and jerked as the van sped down the unpaved road, hitting dips that at times tossed them over six inches off the floor of the van. At times, they both fell on top of each other. They traveled for what seem like hours before the van came to a stop, throwing them both forward. Agent Adams's wound had been treated, the bleeding had stopped; the only thing now was to keep it clean so it would not get infected. They heard the doors being opened, the air was starting to get cool. Agent Adams knew the sun was starting to set as he felt the wind on his face. He had been in this part of the world several times, so he could just about tell what time of the day it was. They were pulled from the van and shoved inside the building; they had taken about twenty steps when they were pulled by the back of their shirts, making them stop dead in their tracks. President Wilkins could feel the cold metal of the iron bars on his face, as they removed their blindfolds and the rope taken off their wrist.

Agent Adams stumbled, and the president grabbed him by the arm to keep him from falling. He eased him to the floor as the door was slammed behind them. President Wilkins sat down next to him and asked him how he felt. "My leg hurts, but it's not bleeding."

"Well, we will have to try to keep it as clean as possible. You don't want that to get infected," the president said with concern. Agent Adams looked around and noticed that they were not alone.

The armed men left them and went outside. He took this time to try and talk to whoever else was in here with them. "Who's there?" he said, trying to not to raise his voice too loud. He heard a young male voice say, "My name is James. There are four of us. Megan is in the cell with me, and Sandra and Karen are in the cell over there.

"Who are you, guys?" James asked.

"My name is Rick Adams."

"Who is that with you?" James said, as he got closer to the cell door so he could get a good look at the men. "I know you, sir. I have seen you before!"

"Me?" Agent Adams asked. "No, the guy with you! He looks like the president." There was silence for several seconds. "That is correct," the president said. "How long have you been here?"

"About a week!" Megan said. "We haven't left the building since we were brought here," Sandra chimed in. Karen asked, "If they can kidnap the president with armed guards, what chance do we have of getting out of here?"

"Have they said anything about what they want?"

"No," James said, "but I guess it would be for a ransom. Someone can't keep her mouth shut and is always telling strangers about who her father is." Megan gave him that shut-up look, then tears started to trickle down her cheeks. "I'm sorry," she said. "I'm sorry. I feel like this is my entire fault."

"It's not," James said, as he put his arm around her, "you just tend to tell perfect stranger all about your family. You just can't trust everybody."

"I know that now," she said softly. "How will we get out of here?" Sandra asked. "Surely, they will send the military here now that you're here, sir, right!"

"I'm not supposed to be here," the president said. "It doesn't matter now," Adams said. "But I did manage to get out a distress call before we were captured. Just don't know if anyone heard it, didn't have time to listen for a response. But if it did, help should be on the way soon," he said with confidence. The president leaned forward and asked, "Did one of you say your name was Megan?"

"Yes, sir, I am Megan Green."

"Well, that's interesting! I was just in a meeting with some of the leaders here discussing your whereabouts. I was trying to negotiate your release."

"On the way back from the meeting, we were ambushed, and we are the only ones that survived," Adams said. "What have they been feeding you, guys?" Adams asked. "Water, bread, and some kind of meat; didn't want to eat it at first," James said, "but after a while, when you get hungry enough, we didn't have a choice. It was that or starve. They let us go to the bathroom. It is by that door over there. It has one guard usually and one by the door you came in."

"How many men have you seen," Adams said.

"Four at one time in here; haven't seen more than that, but I'm sure there are more than that," Sandra said. "You can hear them talking outside and someone is on the roof; we can hear them walking around."

The guards came back inside and heard them talking and told them in broken English to shut up and stop talking. Agent Adams looked at the guard and thought to himself "the first chance I get . . ." The guard looked back at him and gave him a evil look that said, "If you try to cause trouble, you will be shot," as he pointed his AK-47 at him and said, "Bang."

CHAPTER TEN

The Flight

ALL OF THE team members were in the hangar preparing for the mission, they were all talking among themselves when the side door of the hangar opened. Thomas walked in first and behind him was Eva. Everyone stopped talking, and the men looked at Eva, wondering what she was doing there. "Gentlemen, good morning," he said as he and Eva walked past the men. Oscar walked up to them and asked Thomas, "What is Eva doing here?"

"SHE IS GOING with us this time, Oscar!"

"WHAT!"

"LOOK, GUYS, THIS is the deal. Last night, there was an attempt on her life. I am not going to leave her here without protection; so she is going with us. She is more than capable of holding her own."

THEY STARED, AND some of them mumbled among themselves, saying, "She will get in the way. What will she be doing?"

"GENTLEMEN, GATHER AROUND first. Let's get something straight. I have worked with all of you before. I know I can trust you and you guys know you can trust me. Eva is going with us, and that is all there is to it. Now we have another situation. Eva go ahead and tell them."

"ALL RIGHT," SHE said, "on the way over here, we received another mission, and this one is the most important one we will ever have." She paused for a minute as she surveyed the team. "Well, what is it?" Willy said. Eva paused for a second more, then she spoke. "The president has been kidnapped; it happened on Wednesday. His convoy came under attack; nineteen of the twenty guards protecting him were killed. So we have been hired to bring him back, and this has to be done by Monday. He has to be back in the United States by this time like nothing happened. Plus, we still have to save Peter Green's daughter. One good thing about this, believe it or not, they are all in the same place. Now this means that there will be more guards on the building where they are being held."

Most of the men could not believe what they were hearing. "Wait, wait, hold on; how could this be without this being all over CNN!" Lyle said. "And why us? They could have sent in the Marines, do you know what this means for us, and what we'll have to face now?" he said raising his voice, Thomas walked over to Lyle. "The reason they didn't do this is, because if they were to send in a large force, this could easily start a war that would tear apart this region. So we are to get in and get out just like we always do, if anyone wants out, I understand, but for me I am going and so is Eva." They both turned around and picked up their gear and started loading it on the plane; the men looked at each other and started grinning and one by one started moving toward the plane and loading their gear also. Steve walked up to Eva and Thomas and said, "Well, you know we are with you, Thomas, and you know we have overcome some tremendous odds on some of our missions. You know, once they find out that we have the president, they will throw everything but the kitchen sink at us."

"I know," Thomas said, "I will explain once we get in the air what we will have to do to improve our chances of surviving this one."

Eva looked up at Thomas. "What do you think our chances are?"

"We don't think about that when we are out in the field, Eva We just do our jobs and that improves everyone chance of making it back. Come on, let's finish getting the equipment on the plane so we can get under way; timing will be everything on this job, we have about another hour before we leave, so let's double-check the equipment," he said to the team. They all moved quickly and quietly, not much was said as they continued to load the plane. Thomas looked at his watch, twenty minutes to go, all but a few crates were on board. Several of the men tied straps around the two crates, hooked them up to a wench and began to bring them on board. We're making good time, Thomas thought to himself. Even though this was the first part of the mission, it is so important that everything goes as close to the plan as possible. Everything was on board, and Willy had made his final round of the hangar to make sure everything was on board; he walked up the ramp and gave a thumbs-up sign. Thomas picked up the phone that was connected to the cockpit. "We have a green light; let's get this party started." The ramp began to rise up as the plane's engines roared to life. It taxied down the runway and started to gain speed and then lifted up they are now underway.

The C-130 was cold and was not the most comfortable plane to ride on. They were already six hours into the flight when Thomas stood up and said, "All right let's do an equipment check one more time. We will be refueled in the air so this will be a long flight; we will be jumping from thirty-five thousand feet, check your chutes, mask, and oxygen bottles to make sure they are all working. Eva I will check yours."

"That's okay, I got it."

The men watched as she went through her equipment; she then pulled out her Ar-15 assault rifle and proceeded to modify it with the Beowulf (modified to shoot 50-cal rounds). She looked up, because she could feel all eyes were on her. "What? You think I wouldn't pick up some of Thomas's bad habits!" The team smiled and nodded their approval. After the equipment check they began to make themselves as comfortable as they could to get; some sleep before the jump. Thomas put his hand to his throat. "Mike, wake us in fifteen minutes before we jump."

"Roger that," the voice replied. He leaned back and closed his eyes and went through the mission in his mind then drifted off to sleep. Eva looked at the men. How could they go to sleep? She was to nervous; this was the first time for her, and she had no idea of what to expect, but after a few minutes, she found her eyes getting heavy, and she found herself drifting off just like the rest of the team. The sound of engines, as oddly as it seemed, relaxed her, just like a mother humming a lullaby to a baby; the plane ride was pretty smooth; nothing like she had thought.

CHAPTER ELEVEN

"Here we go"

ALL RIGHT, GENTLEMEN, fifteen minutes to drop zone, I repeat, fifteen minutes to drop zone!" Thomas was already awake and stretching. He gave Eva a gentle nudge; she stirred, sat up, and rubbed her eyes. "How long before we jump?"

"WE HAVE ABOUT twelve minutes," he replied. The rest of the team was up and started stretching also. "Ten minutes!" Thomas said. They all began to put on their parachutes and helmets. Eva was amazed at how the men could go from what seem like a dead sleep to being wide awake and sharp. Thomas held up three fingers (three minutes). It was almost time, and Eva was getting more and more nervous. She felt a hand on her shoulder. She turned around; it was one of the team members. She couldn't remember his name. "It's all right. Just take a couple of deep breaths and try to relax." She turned back to see Thomas and five others jumping first. Through her earpiece, she heard "one minute"; her legs felt like rubber, the ramp was still open, the night air was freezing, it was so dark. The crates went next. They seemed to disappear into the abyss. She heard the words "go, go!" It was time; the men began to jump two, three at a time. It was her turn now; she looked at the person next to her. He gave her the thumbs-up sign and grabbed her by the arm. She closed her eyes at first; after about five seconds, she opened them, and she thought this was the closest she was going to get to flying. She began to relax; she looked over. She could see two other team members. They were about five feet from her. She felt so free. This isn't bad at all, she thought. She looked at her altimeter: 3,500 feet. It was time to open her chute; it yanked her back up, and then she began to float. It was quiet, so peaceful, she thought to herself. She looked down to see five chutes opened; the team was split into two groups: Thomas took Willy, Oscar, Lyle, and Steve plus two other team members. The rest of the team will go to the Alamo and make preparations; at least this part was going okay. Even with the chute slowing her descent, the ground was coming up at her pretty fast, she thought, as she prepared for the impact.

She landed with a thump; knees bent, she rolled to keep the impact from causing any injury. She looked around for a second. "I made it," she said to herself. "I made it." Then she heard a voice through here earpiece: "Let's go, people, we have a lot to do and a short time to do it." Thomas's group landed four miles farther east, about two miles from the town where the hostages are being held. His team gathered in a semicircle with their rifle at the ready. Thomas waved his hand forward. "Let's move, people." They moved without saying a word. The team covered the two miles effortlessly and stopped about one hundred yards away from the town. Thomas held up his fist, and the team stopped and lay flat on their stomachs; he pulled out his binoculars. Just as the intel said, there were two men on the roof, one by the front door. But there were a lot more soldiers at the opposite end of the town than he had thought had been in the intelligence report he was given. Instead of fifty, there was more like a couple of hundred. Farther down the road, he could see another camp; this wasn't in the report. He had two other men with the team. "When did they get here! Damn it!" Thomas didn't like surprises like this bad intel made for serious trouble on a mission; the other camp is about two miles away. "Okay, you two circle around you should find a box hidden around the bend in the road there. It should contain some claymores, some land mines, and some antitank and antipersonnel mines in it. Plant them along the road; see if you can put some of claymores by that tanker. That should slow them down in case they come down the road to help them out in case things get a little dicey, also put some claymores there around the machine guns and some under their vehicles; you should be able to get close, the wind is gusting and kicking up a lot of sand. That should give you some cover to get there and get out, we will give you twenty minutes to get back here to help cover the street for our exit. Got it? We will meet you back here." Looking through his binoculars, he could see that there are also buildings to the left that had soldiers coming in and out. "Just great how many soldiers are housed in there?" Now another truck was arriving and pulled up to the building to the right; it was straight across from where the other hostages are being held. The driver got out along with another solider; they walked around to the back of the truck. Then he could see seven women being pushed and pulled toward the building and shoved inside. "What the hell is going on here!" Steve said, looking at Thomas. "Is this hostage depot! Well, more hostages; can't tell if they are American or not; all women and we don't know where they came from or why they are here, it looks like things are about to get more interesting!"

"They are not part of the plan, Thomas!" Steve said. "We can't leave them!" Oscar said, interrupting their conversation. "If we get the others out and leave them, you know they will take it out on them! It looks like we have a change of plans, gentlemen," Lyle chimed in. They all looked at each other and nodded in agreement. "Okay now, this is how we handle this. Steve, you cover us with the MK 11 sniper rifle (this rifle is one of the favorite of the men it is also a semi-automatic with a ten—or twenty-round magazine and uses the Magnum Universal Night Scope has a range of 800 yards and uses the 7.62 x 51 mm NATO round); James, you and Willy check out the building with the women in it; if there are no guards, get them out and hold them there until we rescue the others. Myself and Oscar will go through the front. Lyle, you will go through the back door; the other two will cover the street. Steve, when we get to the first truck, that will be your signal to take out the two guards on the roof. We will need the extra trucks down there, so let's do this quietly and quickly as possible and get out of there before anyone notices us. All right, let's go." They all pulled out their compressors and put them on their rifles, and then made their way down to the camp, moving like predators ready to pounce on its prey.

Eva was back at the Alamo, watching the men making preparations. She felt out of place; one of the men came up to her and said, "Everyone works here!" And he handed her a shovel; she looked at it and then back to him. "We need to make some sandbags; you fill them, and I will put them over there. We are almost done; we just need to make a few more to put in front of the machine gun there." He pointed behind her; she could see it mounted with sandbags and some brush covering it; looked pretty natural, she thought, you almost couldn't see it until he pointed it out to her. They finished making the rest of the sandbags pretty fast. She put the shovel down and began to check out the rest of the Alamo. It was a rock formation that stood some eighty feet in height. It had a large opening, big enough to drive a truck through. She walked through the opening and past the machine gun she had helped make the sandbags for. She looked at it; it was down in a trench that was about four feet deep and about four feet wide it was loaded and ready to fire. Eva walked through the opening to the right. There were two men working on securing what looked like SAMs (surface-to-air missiles). There were at least six that she could see. To the left, there was what looked like tarp covering another opening. She pulled back the tarp to see what seemed to be another opening. It was kind of a shallow cave that went back about twenty feet and was about fifteen feet wide. It was tall enough for her to stand up in. There were sleeping bags and propane lamp and heater, some canned food in one corner. *Hmmm,* she thought to herself. This seems odd, usually the team is in-out of their missions in a matter of hours. She pushed back the tarp and walked out. She looked back to her left to see some men setting up six M252 81mm mortars (they had a minimum range of eighty meters and a maximum of 5,700 meters, and deliver a devastating barrage of explosives), then turned back to the right and saw some more brushes at the base of the slope that went up about two-thirds of the way with what looked a trail of some sort. She walked over and started to walk up the trail when she noticed to her left covered by the brush was another opening. She peeked inside to see twin mounted antiaircraft guns with two large drums on each side. *What in the world was Thomas expecting to happen here.* She stepped out and walked up about thirty feet, and she saw another opening. She looked in and saw a Vulcan M134 minigun; this could fire 3,000 rounds a minute. She then continued up the trail until she reached the top. There were two positions protected by sand bags; she walked over and looked in both; they were each about four feet deep. This area was a hundred yards away from the top of the trail; Eva looked around and noticed three tarps covering something that was about ten feet long and five feet tall. She started walking toward them when she was called back by one of the men. Eva stopped and looked back at the young man who was calling her and looked back to take one more glance at the tarps. The young man called her again; this time, there were two other men standing there with him, and they began to walk her way. She walked past the two men to the young man that was summoning her. She looked back one more time to see the other two men covering the tarps with brush. *What was going on here? How bad is this going to get?* The two of them made their way back down the trail and back through the opening to the Alamo. The young man that was walking with her did not say a word; they had walked some fifty yards away when he stopped and turned around and looked up. There were men high up on the front of the of the Alamo, pulling up three more Vulcan miniguns, one was on the left, one in the middle, and the other was to the right.

She turned around to see several figures working off in the distance covering what looked like barrels with sand and brush. The mortars she saw were M252 81 mm extended range mortars. They had a range of about three miles. Now she was starting to realize why Thomas called this the Alamo. He knew something bad was going to come their way, but just how bad was it going to be? She sat on a large rock that she was standing next to and took a deep breath. Eva was starting to realize that this was going to be fight for their lives; how in the hell are they going to get out of this one? She knew Thomas and his team were good, and they had overcome some incredible odds. What were they going to face this time? She tapped the butt of her AR 15 with her trigger finger and began to check to make sure it was loaded and ready to go. She needed to make sure she was ready and didn't want to let the team down. It was now 10:30 p.m. She was wondering how the team was doing on rescuing the hostages, and when they would make their way back here with the rest of the team.

CHAPTER TWELVE

THE TWO MEN that Thomas sent around to plant the land mines reached the bend in the road and found the box covered with sticks and dirt. It was exactly where Thomas said it would be. The two men worked quickly, not saying a word; this part of the road was dark, and it was perfect for what they were doing. They finished laying the landmines and took the four claymores mines and made their way back. The wind was kicking up enough sand, so they were not seen as they put one on the tanker Thomas had shown them earlier. They made their way to the machine guns, they planted one in front of each machine gun. There was one antiaircraft gun, and they managed to put one there also. The two men hurriedly made their way back to the other end of the town, carrying the remote detonators for the claymores. Thomas gave them twenty minutes to get this done; since there were only eight mines in the box, it took them the full twenty minutes. Steve was watching the two men through his scope on his rifle. This mission was going good so far. Thomas and Oscar were in position by the first truck; Lyle had made his way to the back door. Thomas heard Lyle through his earpiece, "I'm in position."

"ROGER THAT."

"STEVE, WE ARE at the front door."

THOMAS SAW THE two men he sent to plant the explosives making their way to the parked trucks. James and Willy had made their way to the building where the women are being held. There wasn't a guard outside; Willy peeked inside through a small window on the side of the building, and he could see one guard sitting by the door. He appeared to be asleep. He could make the shot from here without busting through the front door. "Thomas, this is Willy. We are in position."

"OKAY, STEVE, ON the count of three, take out the two guards. Three, two, one." Steve's first shot caught the first guard in his left eye; his head jerked backed, and he was dead before he hit the ground. The second guard turned and saw his fellow guard go down before he could act; his fate was the same, he caught a bullet in the forehead, and he too slumped to the ground.

"They're down," Steve said through his throat mike. "Lyle, we have to enter at the same time, on three."

"Roger that." Once again, Thomas counted down, "Three, two, one." Lyle opened the back door about two feet; he spotted the guard standing there. The guard was startled by the door opening; by the time he realized it wasn't one of his own, Lyle had put three shots into him, two to the chest and one to the head. Thomas and Oscar burst through the front door; two guards were there, one in a chair and the other standing next to him. Thomas shot the one standing twice; both rounds caught the man in the forehead. He hit the wall and then slid down, leaving a trail of blood on the wall. Oscar got the one in the chair while he was reaching for his rifle; three quick shots in the chest. The man slumped over and then fell out of his chair. "Lyle," Oscar yelled, "clear," as they made sure the guards were dead. Thomas went over to the first cell where the president and Agent Adams were being held. "Mr. President, we are American soldiers here to rescue you." The president stood up and helped Agent Adams to his feet. "He has been shot in the leg. The bleeding has stopped, but it needs to be cleaned."

"Can he walk?" Adams said, "Yes, just get us out of here." Oscar and Lyle opened the other two cells. Megan and James jumped to their feet. They were more than ready to go. They had been there over a week. Sandra and Karen rushed through the cell door and hugged Lyle and Oscar. "Is everyone okay?" Thomas asked. They all shook their heads okay. "We have to move and move fast. I will go out first and make sure the way is clear. Mr. President, I need you to stay close. Oscar, make sure the kids keep quiet and stay low. Lyle, what are you doing?"

"Setting up a little something for when they find out they're gone." He had rigged a grenade to the back door so when someone opened, they will get quite a surprise; he then followed them out the front door.

Once outside, they were able to get the president and Agent Adams and the kids on the first truck, Thomas had waved for James and Willy to bring the seven women over that were in the other building when he heard a shout. He turned around to see one of the soldiers; they have been spotted, Steve saw the man in his scope and fired, catching the man between the shoulders blades, and he took about two more steps and then fell face-first to the ground. The two men that had planted the explosives were in the first two trucks; they started and black smoke poured out of the exhaust. Thomas ran to the building they had just rescued the president from and took up a defensive position. Oscar did the same on the other side of the street. The guard that Steve shot was able to raise the alarm, and soldiers seem to be coming from everywhere. "Just great," Thomas muttered to himself. Willy ran to the first truck and got the detonators and ran back; there were four of them. He just grabbed the first one and set off the first charge; it exploded in front of the first machine gun, knocking the men back as they were riddled with steel ball bearings that were packed in the claymores. Willy grabbed two more and set them off at the same time; one took out the second machine gun and the other tore about five soldiers to shreds and severely wounded several others. He grabbed the last one and it set off the tanker that was filled with fuel; it lit up the whole camp, setting some of the soldiers on fire. They ran and screamed, as their flesh was melting from the burning fuel on their skin and uniforms.

Thomas raised AA-12 (automatic assault shotgun that uses high explosives frag rounds, slugs and double 00 buckshot; he had thirty-two-round drums of each). The first rounds he used were the explosive rounds. The rounds hit with so much devastation even he couldn't believe how much damage it caused. The rounds were tearing the soldiers to pieces. Some try to run for cover, but it was no use. The rounds were just destroying everything they came in contact with. Thomas switched to the magnum slugs rounds that are capable of going through an engine block. He slid the thirty-two-round drum in and began to fire; it was literally putting holes in men the size of a softball. It was incredible how much devastation this one gun can cause. Oscar was laying down his own onslaught from his assault rifle that uses 50-caliber rounds. The soldiers were coming out of the building where some of them were sleeping. Thomas's men were laying down such firepower they were actually cutting down the soldiers like a lawn mower cutting grass. There were very few soldiers left in the camp; they had taken most of them out. "Let's move," Thomas said. They all made their way back to the trucks; the first truck had the president and the kids, the second truck had the seven women, the last truck Oscar with Thomas, Willy, and Lyle climbing on, still firing at what was left of the soldiers. Oscar looked, and he could see tanks starting to come down the road. When the first one hit the land mine, it exploded, black smoke poured from its frame as it slowly rolled off the road. Another came around the bend, it caught the same fate as the first one; it rolled and hit another land mine and it exploded into flames. A third vehicle came around the bend, swinging wide to avoid the burning tanks and pulled back on to the road, and the back end must have hit the mine, as the rear end lifted up and came down, throwing the driver out and he landed in heap on the side of the road. Steve covered their escape, shooting anything that moved; this kept what was left of the soldiers moving cautiously from one spot to another to keep from getting hit from the sniper fire.

They pulled up to where Steve was; he couldn't believe the damage such a few men could cause, but he could also see they were trying to regroup and send soldiers after them. Four trucks made their way around the bend in the road. "Thomas we are going to have company." The trucks took off, bouncing all over the place as they sped down the dirt road. "We may have five minutes, ten at the most, before they come after us," Steve said to Thomas. "We have a little surprise for them," Thomas said, as he grabbed the satellite phone from Oscar's backpack. "This is Predator One to Safe Haven, this is Predator One to Safe Haven."

"This is Safe Haven, go ahead Predator One."

"We have the packages, is our package ready?"

"Roger that, Predator One, they are two about fifty yards off on both sides of road hidden behind the shrubs; you will know when you see it"

"Got it." The trucks bounced and jerked for about five more minutes before they came to a stop. The driver jumped out. President Wilkins asked "why are we stopping," as he walked past the back of the truck. Thomas and Willy jumped out. Thomas told the drivers to go down the road about two miles and "we will meet you there." Once again, the president asked, "WHY ARE WE STOPPING?"

"Mr. President, one of my men spotted some trucks that were making an attempt to follow us. They maybe five or ten minutes behind us. We have to slow them down." James, Megan, Karen, and Sandra were terrified. They had never experienced anything like this; they didn't say a word. Willy saw the kids' faces, and he knew that they were scared. "It will be okay," he said, smiling at them. "Okay, get them out of here," Thomas said. They stepped back as the trucks rolled past. "Okay which side of the road do you want?" Willy asked. "Doesn't matter to me," Thomas replied. "Where did they put our surprise packages?"

"Well, it is behind some shrubs." And seeing that there were only a few shrubs clumped together on each side, that must be it. They both ran toward the shrubs. Willy went to the right, and Thomas went to the left; they both found the equipment quickly. Both packages included an M60 machine gun with 500 rounds and RPG (rocket propelled grenade) with three rockets. Thomas put the first rocket in the RPG and loaded his M60. Willy was doing the same on his side of the road. "Willy are you ready for this?" he said through his throat mike. "Roger that." Thomas looked through his binoculars; he could see four trucks coming down the road. Just about what he thought after that ass-kicking they just took back at the camp, this was all they were going to send until they made sure there was no more land mines or booby trap on the road. "Okay, I will take out the first two trucks, and you take out the last two, then we will hit them with the M60s . . . Predator One to Safe Haven."

"This is Safe Haven."

"Any word on the helicopters yet?"

"Not yet, Predator One, unable to raise them on the com link yet."

"Great, they should have been on their way so we can get out of here. "Keep trying, Predator One, out." The trucks were getting closer now; he raised his RPG and took aim at the first truck. First, the seven extra hostages they rescued, and now they haven't heard from the helicopters, things were starting to go bad after that firefight in the camp, and he was sure they knew the hostages were gone. He was sure they will throw whatever they have at them to get the hostages back, especially the president. This mission was going to hell fast, he thought, as the first truck was about fifty yards away. "Well, here we go." He fired the RPG at the first truck.

CHAPTER THIRTEEN

EVA HEARD THE news over the radio that Thomas and his team had gotten the hostages out; now they had to make their way back here. She heard about the firefight plus you could hear it even though they were miles away; sounds travel a long way when it is quiet like it was tonight. She and the men at the camp looked out into the desert, and they could see flashes of light and explosions off in the distance; no doubt they had run into more trouble, and if they make it back, how many troops will be following behind them? "All right, let's get the second trap ready; they should be coming through here shortly, and we need to have everything ready."

"WHERE DO YOU want me?" Eva asked. "How about you backing up the 50-cal in the middle. He will need you to cover him while he reloads." There were three staged areas that housed the machine guns: one on the left and the right, and the one she will assist with is the one in the middle. All hell was about to break loose; to the far left, about sixty or seventy yards out and the same to the right, were trenches about four feet deep, and each one had two RPGs (with five rounds each) spaced about twenty yards apart in the trenches. This ambush area was just below a small ridge. If anything came over that, it would be caught by surprise, and the ambush must be made for tanks or armored vehicles that come over the ridge. If you catch a tank with an RPG from the underneath, it was a clear kill shot. The machine guns had to be for troops and any light vehicles that will be supporting the tanks. She got into position by the 50-cal in the middle; she checked her assault rifle and her Sig Sauer pistol to make sure everything was in working order and that she had plenty of ammo for both. The guy that was manning the 50-cal was checking it to make sure it was working properly. He looked at her and smiled and gave her a thumbs-up.

CHAPTER FOURTEEN

THOMAS HIT THE first truck right where the troops were sitting in the back of truck; the explosion knocked some of the men out on other side. The unfortunate ones that were on the side the rocket hit were not so lucky. It blew body parts all over the back of the truck; some of the soldiers died instantly. Others were screaming, looking at missing limbs and their life blood seeping from their wounds. Willy fired his RPG, catching the last truck that had stopped and was trying to back up; the rocket must have hit the fuel tank. It exploded in a great fireball that lit up the night. Soldiers fell from the wreckage in flames; they didn't have a chance. Thomas fired his second rocket; it hit the cab of the second truck, killing the driver instantly. The soldiers that survived the blast jumped out and tried to find cover where ever they could. Willy fired again, hitting the vehicle close to the back wheels, causing it to jump up three feet and landing in a heap. The men that made it through the blast bailed out of the truck and ran for cover and shot wildly in all directions. Thomas fired his last rocket in between the burning wreckage, catching some of soldiers who were lying as close as they could get to the ground. The rocket hit the ground, sending rocks and shrapnel flying all over and hitting some of them. The rocket did its job, maiming several and killing others. Willy also fired his last rocket, catching some of the soldiers from behind who thought they had found cover from the barrage of rocket fire. The rocket hit with deadly effect, tossing two men in the air. They landed in a bloody heap; another soldier was cut in half and two more thrown about five feet but were still able to fight. Thomas and Willy then opened fire with their M60 machine guns with short burst; the soldiers tried to scramble for more cover, trying to hide behind anything they thought would keep them out of harm's way. Then some of them tried to make a run for it. Willy leveled the M60 and cut loose with a five-second burst that cut them down; their bodies twisted, flopped, and then fell to the ground. Willy kept firing until he was out of ammo. Thomas held his fire. There was about ten seconds of silence. What was left of the soldiers got up and made a run for it, as they cleared the last burning truck. Thomas swung his M60 in their direction and opened fire. He caught three of them, knocking the men off their feet; one landed on his side, one almost did a complete flip and landed on his neck and shoulder. The third one seemed to be trying to hold his chest, as he stumbled a few feet, fell to his knees and then landed face-first in the dirt. Just as the third one fell, three more ran from behind the truck sprinting like track stars. It was hard trying to get a bead on them, as they zigzagged. Thomas opened fire; bullets were zipping all around them. Thomas decided to just fire until he was out of ammo. One of them fell and got back up and kept running. Thomas kept firing, the bullets kicked up dirt and rocks all around them. These guys could have outrun Carl Lewis. He hit another one around the shoulder; he spun around, fell, rolled, and was back on his feet and running in a full sprint back toward the direction they had came from. Thomas was out of ammo; three had got away and no doubt they will tell whoever is in charge back at the camp, and they will send more soldiers, this time better equipped. Thomas was sure of it. "Willy let's set a little something for them when they come back through. I'm sure they will check these areas where we have been firing from."

"WILL DO."

THOMAS SET A hand grenade in the RPG, pulled the pin and set it up on its end if someone was to pick it up, it would explode instantly. Willy set his under the empty ammo can that held the rounds for the M60; if this was picked up or knocked over, it would set it off.

They both met back on the road gave each other a high five and started running to meet up with the rest of team. They had run for some five minutes or so before they caught up with the team. Steve, Oscar, and Lyle were standing next to the last truck, as Thomas and Willy came running up. They all had big grins on their faces. "I wouldn't smile too much," Willy said, "three of them got away and I'm sure they will be more coming this time and better equipped," They all climbed in the truck and drove off. "What will happen next?" Agent Adams said. "Well, we have to get you and the president and the kids back to the Alamo."

"The Alamo?" Agent Adams said. "Well, that's what we call it; that will be our last line of defense," Willy said, "we haven't heard from the helicopters yet to get everyone picked up." Thomas picked up the satellite phone. "Hey, get the president and the kids back to the Alamo and have the doc check them out. Is everything else set up for the second round?"

"Yes, sir!" the voice said on the other end. "What are you expecting?" Agent Adams asked. "Another attack," Lyle said, "they will definitely attack again, this time they will hit us harder. I'm sure they are pretty pissed over us, rescuing the hostages and killing a high number of their soldiers, and they are going to throw everything but the kitchen sink at us; so, we have a couple of surprises for them when they come, and believe me, they will come."

CHAPTER FIFTEEN

THE THREE SOLDIERS that got away made their way back to the camp; two of them wounded and the third one was tired and covered in blood from helping the other two. They were greeted by several of their comrades who helped them into one of the buildings where they could receive medical care. The news spread fast through the camp that they were there and what happened to the soldiers that were with them. The leader of soldiers heard the rumors and went to see the men for himself and to find out how only three out of fifty men made it back. When he made his way to the building, he walked through the door. Everyone in the room stood at attention. The leader was tall man, dark with dark eyes and a mingle grey beard, and two scars one over his left eye and the other one ran four inches down his right cheek. He was a battle-hardened leader who had been in many battles in the Middle East. He made his way over to the three men who were being treated for their wounds; a chair was brought over so he could sit down. He began to ask the men what happened and how they survived. Were they cowards? Did they fight honorably? The third soldier who helped the other two wounded men sat up and began to tell what they had encountered; he couldn't tell how many men attacked them. It just seemed they were everywhere. They were hit by RPGs and machine gun fire that seem to come from all sides. The leader left the men and walked out of the building; whoever these soldiers are that took the hostages were very experienced and well armed. He called for all of his military leaders he had; together, they have to be caught.

They made a plan to send eight tanks and 200 troops and six M113 light armored vehicles within the hour, hoping to catch the rescuers by surprise and make them pay for what they did to his men; he told the attacking force to show no mercy. The group was checking their weapons and loading extra ammo for the tanks and the soldiers. They were making sure they would not be caught like the other men were earlier.

It was close to midnight when Thomas and his group got back to their base camp. The trucks pulled up next to the entrance to the huge rock face they called the Alamo. Everyone got out and they were greeted by the rest of the team that was there. Eva ran up to Thomas. "How did it go and was anyone hurt?"

"No, but we sure laid a hurting on the soldiers at that camp, and I'm sure they will send out another patrol, this time bigger and better equipped than the last one."

"What happened? We saw and heard the explosions," Eva said. "They sent out a small force of about fifty men," Willy said, walking between Eva and Thomas. "We killed all but three. Thomas hit two of them, but they got back up and kept running. They probably made it back to their camp, and right now, they are planning or on their way here." One of the other men came up to Thomas and told him that the second stage was set, and they can use one of trucks to take them to the ambush spot. "All right, get the president and the others inside and have them checked out, and make sure you give them something to eat." President Wilkins and Agent Adams entered into the large opening, with the kids, Sandra, Megan, James, and Karen walking close behind. They were amazed at the weapons that they came across; there was six portable TOW missiles and ten Javelin missiles; both are tank-destroying missiles. Agent Adams also noticed the five M252 81mm mortars on the way in, and along the top of the ridge were several men placing FIM-92A shoulder-fired Stinger missiles; they seemed to be preparing for some heavy action. They walked along for some thirty yards and came to a dark tarp. One of Thomas's men pulled back the tarp, and hidden behind it was a fairly large area that had sleeping bags and portable heaters and some canned food. Next to the heaters were two benches. President Wilkins helped the wounded agent down on one of them. The young man that escorted them was a medic and proceeded to clean and redress his wound. "Sir, are you okay?"

"Yes," the president replied, "but you might want to take a look at the kids." He turned to the four teenagers. They said that they were okay, just tired and hungry. They opened two of the cans— corned beef hash and pork and beans. Normally, they wouldn't touch something like this, but under the circumstances, this was as good as bacon and eggs. Megan found a small pan and emptied the contents of the corned beef hash and scraped it into the pan and placed it on the small propane stove she found next to the pan.

After they had eaten, the young man came back and told them they had a place where they can clean up. They all walked outside, and across from where they were was a couple of stands with pots on top full of water and washcloth and soap next to each one. This wasn't much, but it's better than nothing. The men let the girls and women go first, and then they each took turns washing themselves. When they all had finished, they walked back. The men let the ladies have the sleeping bags. Someone had turned on the heaters, and the small area was really pretty cozy now; they all settled in and dozed off. Outside Thomas and his men were getting ready to go the next ambush area to get ready for the next attack they knew for sure was coming. Oscar got behind the wheel of the truck and started it up. "Let's go, we need to get in place!" he shouted from the driver's side window. Eva and Willy got in the cab with Oscar; Thomas, Steve, and Lyle and two other men got in the back. They drove for about five minutes; they came upon the area where they had laid an ambush for the soldiers they knew were coming. There were two trenches about four feet deep and 150 yards across from each other.

At the other end of each trench about fifty yards back were 50-cal machine guns both armed with armor-piercing incendiary rounds.

Willy and Oscar were in one trench about twenty yards apart both armed with RPG-7s with five rounds each, capable of knocking out tanks and light armored vehicles; they both had their Beowulfs (AR-15s modified to shoot 50-cal rounds). Thomas and Lyle had the same on the other side. Steve and Eva were manning one 50-cal, and the other two men were manning the other. "This should make for one hell of a kill zone," Steve said to Eva. She had never seen anything like this; she was scared. "Nervous?"

"No, more like scared to death."

"It's okay. We usually are too."

"So how do you handle it?"

"Let me ask you a question, Eva."

"All right."

"What is the difference between a coward and a hero?"

"I don't know!"

"A coward may run or freeze up; a hero, even though he may be scared, will stay and do what is expected of him. When the time comes, take a deep breath and squeeze off your rounds. If you put two rounds center mass, I guarantee that guy will go down. You will be okay. Thomas wouldn't have you come along if he didn't think you could handle it, so just have a seat there and try to relax. When this jumps off, you really don't have time to be scared, you just react." Steve than picked up his binoculars and looked out in the distance. "Nothing yet," he pressed on his throat mike. "Thomas, you see anything yet?"

"No, but keep your eyes open. They may try to send in a small team first to try and to get us to give away our positions."

"Roger that."

CHAPTER SIXTEEN

IT WAS 12:30 a.m. The leader got into the lead tank, a Russian T-72. It was equipped with an 840-hp diesel engine. It is armed with 125mm smoothbore gun with an effective range of 2000 meters and a 7.62mm machine gun, plus a 12.7 mm NSV antiaircraft machine gun. But to fire this gun, the tank commander has to be halfway out of the turret, which makes him susceptible to snipers. He lead the force out of the camp on what he thought would be a fairly easy task of catching the men that rescued the prisoners (but he had no idea of what he and his men were in for). They traveled down the same road taken by the first four trucks that were destroyed, except that they were spread out about one hundred yards wide with the eight tanks and the M113s leading the way. The 200 men were in seventeen trucks following close behind. Whatever they ran into, they would be ready this time (so he thought, but would soon find out differently). They rumbled across the wide open country. They had pretty good visibility, except when the wind would gust that caused dirt to swirl and knocked down their visibility considerably.

Willy was looking off in the distance with his binoculars when he spotted them. Thomas and Steve spotted them at the same time. "Thomas, are you seeing this!"

"Yes! I see five, six, no wait, eight tanks and several light armored vehicles; I count six of those, and about twenty trucks. Probably filled with soldiers at least twelve per truck that would put it at 200 or more soldiers. Well, here we go, they should reach us in about ten minutes. All right, people, stay low until they are within range." Thomas's voice was calm. "How can he be like that in a time like this?" Eva asked Steve. "It keeps the rest of at ease. You see, if you panic, you make careless mistakes, and if you make careless mistakes, that could lead to people getting hurt or killed."

The leader was watching the area through his binoculars; nothing out of the ordinary. *Where are these sorry dogs that killed his men and took the hostages?* He could feel the anger swell in him building to a peak. *When I catch up with them, they will pay and pay dearly*, he muttered through clenched teeth, and his jaws tightened.

They were getting close. Willy could hear and feel the sounds of the tanks rumbling toward them; any minute now they will fall into the ambush that was set for them. The tanks were at the top of the ridge and were coming down. You could hear Thomas say, "Easy, easy, wait for it. FIRE." The first rocket found its mark just below the turret on the tank closest to him. The armor-piercing round penetrated the tank's armor. It exploded, blowing the turret half off, and it rolled to a slow stop (seven more to go). Willy fired from his position, hitting one of the tanks from behind; it burst into flames, Oscar fired his rocket and another tank went up in flames, Lyle fired and another one went down. The leader was caught by surprise and his crew started to fire wildly with machine gun fire and its 125 mm gun blasting in the direction they thought the missiles were coming from. The last four tanks did the same; exploding shells and machine gun fire filled the air. One of the shells hit between Thomas and Lyle, knocking them off their feet. They were stunned for a few seconds, but were able to gather themselves. Eva and Steve were watching from their position. The night was filled with bright yellow and orange balls of fire. "Why aren't you firing?" she yelled at Steve. "Not yet. We can't give away our positions to them yet," he yelled back at her. Thomas, Lyle, Willy, and Oscar each fired again, and the rest of the tanks exploded. The leader was blown from his tank and landed in a heap on the ground. He was bloodied and semi-conscious. He managed to stand and stagger off away from his burning tank. Just then, the rest of his fighting force came over the ridge, laying down a deadly barrage of machine gun fire. Thomas and his group ducked down in the trenches, as bullets flew all around them. Oscar popped up and fired, catching one of the troop carriers on the side. It exploded, flames and smoke poured out of the vehicle; the men inside didn't have a chance.

Steve opened fire with his 50-cal loaded with armor-piercing incendiary rounds. The bullets cut through the thin armor of the M113 like a hot knife through butter. The vehicle turned sharply and rolled over. The other two positions then opened fire also spitting death with every round that was fired; the soldiers were falling like bowling pins, Willy and Oscar fired the rest of their rockets, Thomas and Lyle did the same with devastating effect. The night sky lit up like a Christmas tree. The leader looked back and could not believe that his men again were being cut to pieces. His light armored troop carriers and trucks were being destroyed faster than anything he had ever seen. Thomas, Lyle, Oscar, and Willy opened fire with their assault rifles. The opposing force didn't have a chance. They couldn't hide anywhere the armored vehicles, and the trucks were trying to retreat but were being ripped to shreds. The leader tried to make a run for it. Thomas spotted him; this time he leveled his rifle and fired six times. All six of the 50-cal rounds found their mark, leaving holes the size of a man's fist in his torso. He fell fast, headfirst. By the time the 50-cal machine guns were through firing, the barrels were glowing red. Eva had used up four thirty-round clips; she couldn't believe what she had just been through. It was quiet now; all you could see was the burning wrecks of tanks, trucks, and the armored troop carriers and the burning of flesh which made Eva sick to her stomach. Back at the base camp President Wilkins and Agent Adams were watching through night-vision binoculars. "Outstanding," Adams said to the president, "these guys really know what they are doing." The nurses were watching from the front entrance of the camp. They saw the sky light up with explosions and wondered how many of the men might be injured. They asked the medic what they could do to help him prepare for the injured. He was leaning against the wall with his arms folded. "No need," he responded. They looked at him with disbelief. "You need some plan of action when the injured get here," one of the nurses yelled at him. "Miss, you have no idea, if anybody needs medical attention, it will not be Thomas and his team; it will be the soldiers they are shooting at!" He turned and walked off; the nurse's stood there bewildered, looking at each other. Five minutes later, the truck that carried Thomas and his team off to the ambush returned. The nurses rushed up to it; all of his team jumped out. The worst injury that occurred were just a few scratches. Eva walked past the nurses. "What happened?" one of them asked. Eva turned to them, shaking her head. "You wouldn't believe it. I have never seen anything like it."

"What do we have to eat? I'm starving," Oscar said. "First, everyone check your weapons and then get something to eat, then get some sleep, the rest of you will be on watch. Is everything else set up? Yes, great. They will try again once they regroup. Any word on the helicopters?"

"Not yet. I don't like this, Thomas," Steve said, "something's not right about this."

"I know," Thomas said, "I know."

CHAPTER SEVENTEEN

OUT OF OVER two hundred men that the leader brought, only a handful made it out alive. They were bleeding from gunshot wounds, several suffered from burns. They managed to get one of the trucks that somehow had just minor damage. They climbed in and began to make their way back to camp; whoever these soldiers were, they now had their ass kicked twice in the same day. They had what seemed like forever to get back to their camp; seven out of over two hundred men, tanks and armored vehicles. How will they explain this to the general? It took them about thirty minutes to get back to their camp. When they pulled up, there were numerous soldiers there now, and they were sure that the general was somewhere in the camp. They came to a stop, sat there for a minute, and then got out; several of their comrades came to their aid and began to ask questions. Where is everyone else? This can't be all? The wounded men just made their way to the aid station to receive medical attention, and all the way there they were asked question after question of what happened. Where is everyone else?

One of the general's aides came in to question the men. Then they began to tell him what happened; after he heard this, he started to ask questions: "You're telling me that out of over two hundred men, eight tanks, and thirteen armored personnel carriers and twenty trucks, just the seven of you survived! How many men did they have?"

"We don't know, sir. It seemed like they were everywhere. Rockets, machine gun fire; they just ripped us to pieces. We didn't have a chance. They were waiting for us, sir. They knew we were coming!" After hearing this, the aide stood up. "I will report back to the general and tell him what has happened here tonight. He will not be happy. The rest of you had better start getting ready. I guarantee he will try again, and this time, he will plan everything himself, and he will come at them hard, and he will not show any mercy!"

CHAPTER EIGHTEEN

THE AIDE LEFT the room and got into his jeep and drove back to report to General Fawwaz (his name means "most successful"), a job he wish he didn't have to do this time. He arrived at the general's office a few minutes later; it was just a few minutes from the smaller camp where the hostages had been held. He walked up to the door and took a deep breath and then knocked. "Come in!" a deep voice said from inside the office. The aide opened the door. The general was looking down at some papers and didn't really acknowledge him at first. He stood there for a minute, then the general looked up at him. "Well!" The aide then began to tell him what had happened. The general was sitting back in his chair, staring at the aide, as he told him what had took place earlier. He then leaned forward and put his hand flat on the desk. "You mean to tell me that out of over two hundred men, only seven lived?"

"YES, SIR!"

"HOW MANY MEN did they come up against?"

"THE STRENGTH OF the opposing force is unknown, general! They have seemed to catch them in an ambush and destroyed all the light armored vehicles and eight tanks, killed over two hundred men."

"HOW MANY DID our men kill?" The aide hesitated, licked his lips nervously. "None."

"NONE, NONE, WHAT do you mean none!" He began to shout at the aide, slamming his fist down on the desk. "How do tanks and two hundred men not hit anything, how is that possible?"

"I DON'T KNOW, General, but that is what the survivors told me."

"SHOW ME ON the map where this took place." The aide walked over to the map on the wall and pointed to the spot on the map. "Very clever," he muttered to the aide. The tanks could not see anything until it was too late. You see here, the ridge kept them hidden until they were almost on top of them; and then firing from different areas probably confused them. Where do you think they are now?" The aide said, "If I were to guess, I would say right here; they don't seem to be moving too fast. That could mean two things, either they are waiting for something or they are on foot."

"WE HAVE TWO encounters with these people and have suffered heavy causalities. What time is it? he asked the aide. "It is about 2:00 a.m., why?"

"GET ALL THE commanders together, we will meet here at my office we will hit them one more time and this time, WE WILL NOT FAIL!"

It took the aide about thirty minutes to get all the commanders together. They were scattered all over the camp. They all met back at the general's office at about 2:35 a.m. The general went through his plan; they will use a full battalion, 28 tanks and about 1,000 men. "We will also have a 15 tanks come up from behind them."

"Will this attack happen simultaneously?"

"Yes!" the general said. "This way, we will CRUSH THEM. I have already sent a messenger to the battalion leader, General Fathi, here." He pointed to a spot on the map. "They are about sixty miles east of us. Our radio is out; that is why I have dispatched a messenger to him. We will move out about 5:00 a.m. We should get there about first light and catch them by surprise.

The messenger was on his way to General Fathi's camp (whose

name means "victorious one"). He has never lost a battle; he was ruthless and cunning. He would surely make sure these soldiers, whoever they are, will not get away. The messenger was rounding a bend in the road when he hit an IED (independent explosive device); shrapnel ripped through the floor board of his jeep, killing him instantly. This would prove costly for General Fawwaz and his men, but will be a blessing for Thomas and his team.

CHAPTER NINETEEN

THOMAS AN D H I S men had everything pretty much ready for the next attack that he knew was coming. He had three men on watch, and everybody else was to get some sleep (that is, if they can). Everyone had eaten, and they were bedding down to get some sleep. The weapons had been checked and rechecked to make sure there were no malfunctions. If Thomas had figured it correctly, they could at least get three hours of sleep. He was quite sure that an attack would happen at first light. He wanted to be up and have everyone in their places and ready to go. This was going to be a fierce battle; he could feel it. The hours passed by quickly. Thomas was up and checking on things. He was walking around the camp one more time to make sure everything was in place. If all goes well, they should be able to hold them off until the helicopters get here.

General Fawwaz and his troops and tanks were now leaving their camp. It was an impressive sight, twenty-eight tanks and one thousand men rumbling toward what they thought would be a victory over these intruders that had taken the hostages and killed so many of his men. This will come to an end today, he was sure of it. Once they see all the firepower coming at them, they were sure to be terrified and surrender or be killed. But he had never faced anything like what he was about to take on. The brigade was moving at a pretty good pace and should make it to their destination by first light, just like the general had planned. He was full of confidence as he looked around at this mighty force. It was sure to strike fear in the hearts and minds of the men he was about to attack. The men on watch saw the brigade coming. With all the dust that were kicking up from the tanks, they knew that this was a big force coming their way. "Thomas, you may want to come up here!" The voice crackled through his earpiece. He responded, "I'm on my way." He made his way up to the area where the men were. He grabbed a pair of binoculars and peered through them. "WOW!" was all he could say. He scratched his chin. "All right, fellas, let's get into position." Steve came up to Thomas and the men who were on watch. "Thomas, we just heard from the helicopters they will be here in twenty minutes. I hope we can hold out that long." Steve grabbed Thomas's binoculars to take a look. "Damn!"

CHAPTER TWENTY

T WAS ALMOST 6:00 a.m. General Fawwaz was coming up on Thomas and his men's position. He was about three miles away. He peered through his binoculars; nothing was moving. He looked from left to right. Twice his men have been caught in ambushes; he was trying to make sure he didn't get caught in one. He couldn't wait until he could spring his trap when these men find out that they are trapped between two forces with no way out. But he was the one that was about to get surprised this day; not knowing that his message did not get through was going to prove fatal this day and that divine intervention was with Thomas and his men today.

The sight of this force has to be intimidating to these men, and they will probably surrender. But the men he was about to face were cool and calculating, and he was about to fall into another trap himself. Thomas had a kill zone of four hundred yards wide. If he could keep these troops in that zone and funnel them into a narrower zone of two hundreds, this would prove devastating to General Fawwaz and his men. Steve, Oscar, Willy, Lyle, and Thomas were all watching now. "Thomas that is a lot of firepower coming our way."

"I know, but you know what is good about this?"

"What?"

"They don't have a clue what is about to hit them. They are already in range of the mortars. We will cut loose with those first. We have five M252 81mm mortars with 30 rounds each. Then they have to go through the minefields there. We have, gentlemen, antitank mines and antipersonnel mines as well. Then after that, they will have to face another surprise!"

"Like what?" Lyle asked.

"If you look right along there, we have fifty barrels of fifty-gallon drums of highly flammable liquid. They are spaced twenty yards apart; they can be set off by a timer that is linked to a laptop. And then, guys, right below where we are now, there are three Vulcan M134 Gatling guns; one below us, one on the right, and one on the left. They all have two 6,000-round drums. There are six TOW missiles and six Javelin tank destroyers missiles. We may not be able to defeat them, but we sure can put quite a hurt on them.'"

"What about attack helicopters or fighter aircraft?" Oscar asked.

"Don't worry, I have something for them; we have five Stinger missiles. I just hope that will be enough!"

"Where do you want us?" Willy asked. "I want you and Oscar and Steve on the miniguns. Lyle, Eva, and I will be on the 50-cal sniper rifles. We only have thirty rounds each on the rifles, so one shot, one kill. Let's get into position." It only took a few minutes for everyone to get into position. Thomas was watching the opposing force get closer. He pressed his fingers against his throat mike. "Mortar crews, OPEN FIRE!" The first deadly salvo of mortar rounds were on the way to their targets.

General Fawwaz was in the lead tank; he heard the whistling sound of the mortar rounds as they made their way toward his men. He quickly closed the hatch on his tank as the first rounds hit the ground close to his tank. He could feel the vibrations of the explosions and sounds of shrapnel hitting the side of his tank. He couldn't see the mortar crews, so they had to be using spotters. Pretty clever, he muttered to himself. He told his tank crews to open fire. The spotters or spotter had to be pinned down; maybe he could knock them out of commission if he kept up a barrage of fire from the 125mm cannons on the T 72. The barrage from the tanks hit the cliff face with incredible force, but the mortar crews kept adjusting, and by the time they fired their fifteenth round, the mortars found their marks with deadly effect. Some hit the tops of the tanks right behind the hatch, killing the commander inside. Others caught the back end of the tanks, destroying the motor and damaging the hydraulic system. The light armored troop carriers were not as fortunate they exploded, killing everyone inside. Those that survived wish they hadn't; they had severe burns. Some were so bad that their skin just slide off as their fellow soldiers tried to pull them from the burning vehicles. This went on for ten minutes, but it seemed like an eternity to these men. Then silence, an eerie silence as the mortars stopped. General Fawwaz opened the hatch of his tank. He rose up slowly to take a look. Five tanks and nine troop carriers destroyed plus the men inside. He radioed the communication truck to see where General Fathi was. "How far away is he?"

"He hasn't left yet, General."

"Why not? Didn't the messenger get there?"

"No!"

"Patch him through to my tank! . . . General Fathi!"

"Yes, General!"

"I had sent a messenger to you; to inform you that we need your assistance!"

"No messenger made it here; what is your situation?"

"We have an unknown number of armed men that attacked our camp, killing over two hundred of my men. What is your location? We are sixty miles east of you."

General Fawwaz explained to General Fahti what had transpired. First, he wanted to know how they got into the region without him knowing about it, and how did General Fawwaz lose so many men and not know who he was up against? This was totally unacceptable to him. Now he was to help him clean up this mess.

"General Fawwaz, I have ten tanks and about five hundred men not too far from you on a training exercise. They heard the artillery and gunfire and figured you were on a training exercise also. I can have them there in thirty minutes or less."

"Thank you, General; now these men will pay for what they have done."

Willy was watching and asked Thomas why have they stopped,. "I don't know Willy! Oscar how much longer before the choppers get here?" "About fifteen minutes."

The general closed the hatch on his tank and told his men to move forward, black smoke from the diesel engines filled the air. They were on the move again. "All right, here we go, they are on the move again." Thomas pressed his throat mike. "Let's get the TOW and the Javelin missiles ready. They still have twenty three tanks left; gentlemen, acquire your targets, we have only twelve missiles, so make them count. With that, the men manning the missiles fired three of the six TOW missiles. The missiles were ejected from the tubes, and when they were a safe distance away, the propellant from inside the missiles was ignited by the small electric motor inside, propelling them toward their targets at a speed of 620 mph. The missiles hit the tanks so fast, the crews didn't have time to react. They exploded, sending the turret some sixty feet, parts flew everywhere after the smoke cleared. All that was left of the three tanks were black spots and pieces of the tanks' track.

This was devastating to the rest of the tank crews, including General Fawwaz. He had never seen a tank explode like that; he gritted his teeth and told the tanks' commanders to fire and keep firing. The tanks let loose an awesome display of firepower. The shells slammed against the rock face, dust and debris flew everywhere. The next three TOW missiles found their marks with the same effect. They seem to disappear in a puff of smoke like a magician doing a magic trick; but this was no magic trick. The tanks just seem to evaporate, just leaving a black spot of where they used to be. Six tanks gone in two minutes. What are they using? General Fawwaz thought to himself. All he could do was tell his men to keep moving forward. The men in the M113 light armored vehicles started to panic and moved in behind the tanks. If those missiles could do that to a tank, they could only imagine what would happen if one of their vehicles got hit. The men prepared the Javelin missiles next. They took a few seconds to acquire their targets and then fired three. The missiles flew up in the air and came down right on the hatch of the next three tanks. One exploded from the inside out like a can of beans under extreme pressure, another tank you could see fire coming from every opening the flames could find. It slowly came to a stop and then exploded. The last tank just seem to spit sparks and flames some ten feet in the air. The 125mm cannon just dropped like a dead tree limb, smoke poured from everywhere then flames. then it exploded. None of the crews had a chance; you couldn't even see any trace of the crew that was inside of the tanks. The men fired the last three Javelin missiles. All three once again found their mark with the same effect. General Fawwaz now had eleven tanks left, and once again, there was silence. Now what? Whoever these men were, they are well prepared, and he was now understanding how they were able to kill over two hundred of his men; these men whoever they are, are very clever, very clever indeed.

CHAPTER TWENTY-ONE

The minefield

THE MINEFIELD WAS about 300 hundred yards from the rock face; the tanks and the armored vehicles were about 400 hundred yards out and closing. Thomas and his men were watching with anticipation; 375 yards out, 350, 325, 310, and then the first tank hit one. A big explosion and a plume of smoke rose from beneath the tank as it came to a stop. Some of the crew inside made their way out of the hatch and jumped off only to step on antipersonnel mines. They were tossed into the air like rag dolls and landed in a heap. One was still alive and screaming in pain as he tried to hold on to what was left of his leg. It was only attached by the smallest piece of flesh and tendons. Ten tanks left, and General Fawwaz was now understanding what the other men had encountered earlier. They bait you into what they want you to do; they are one step ahead of you. It was too late now; he was in the middle of this mess, and he had to figure out how to make it out. You really can't go backward; they had probably accounted for that. So they pushed on with the

125mm cannons firing at the rock face. Hopefully, they can keep them pinned down. The minefield had an incredible effect not only on destroying tanks and armored vehicles; the mental effects it had was even worse. The men were not the most experienced soldiers; they were shocked, confused, and mostly scared at what they had encountered so far.

Their light armored vehicles were being decimated. They started to panic and tried to spread out even farther in hopes of somehow getting out of the minefield. But it seemed no matter which way they went, they ran into one. Some of them stopped and tried to set up some kind of defense. With mortars and rifles, they started to dig in behind their vehicles, as the tanks kept moving forward and firing. Another tank went down, then another. The general was in the middle of hell itself, and there was no way out, but he kept pushing forward. The damage was nothing he had ever seen before. They were about 250 yards away from the rock face. When it happened, the fifty barrels of flammable liquid exploded in front of him. It caught two more tanks. He was down to eight tanks out of twenty-eight. The heat from the fire was incredible. It was so hot inside of the tanks, it was almost unbearable, but he dare not open the hatch of his tank. He tried several times to contact his communication van that was in the rear before he got through; he needed air support, and he needed it now.

CHAPTER TWENTY-TWO

The last stand

THE HELICOPTERS CAME first—two MI-17S, Russian-made. They were equipped with unguided rockets, 12.7mm machine guns and came cruising in at 125 mph. Willy saw them first. "Hey, guys, we have choppers at two o'clock and moving fast." A voice crackled over their earpieces. It was the same guys that handled the mortars and the TOW and Javelin missiles "We got him." General Fawwaz was sure this was a surprise to them, and he figured he finally had the upper hand. A big grin was on his face when they arrived, but it soon turned to a frown. The Stingers were fired and traveling at a speed of over 1,500 mph. The choppers went down just as fast as they appeared; two big balls of fire and falling to the ground in many pieces. "This can't be. Every time, they have an answer for everything we throw at them." Next came two Mirage 2000-Ds French fixed-wing fighter jet carrying two AS-30L laser-guided missiles, each one weighing over 1,100 pounds. The Mirage pilots fired one missile each, both of them hitting the lower part of the rock face. The impact was incredible; everything shook, the noise was deafening. President Wilkins and Agent Adams were knocked off their feet. Megan, Sandra, Karen, and James were terrified. They were all huddled together; the noise from the battle was something they were not used to. Megan was thinking how foolishly they had been to go on this so-called adventure. Now not only are their lives at stake but the men that were here to rescue them also. Her father had always told her the decisions you make not only affect you but also the people around you. People are dying out there because of them. If she lives through this, she will make better decision from now on. She prayed and made a promise to God that she would do better. Funny, in times like this when people think they are going to die how they will pray to God to save them and make promises that they will not probably keep.

General Fawwaz was thinking, now the tide is changing in his favor. The jets came around for the second run on Thomas and his team. This time, the rockets hit close to the top of the rock face. Big pieces of rock and dirt seem to block out the sun for a few seconds; everything was dark. This time, General Fawwaz knew he had the upper hand. Thomas was covered with dirt and other debris from the explosions. It took him a few seconds to gather himself. "Will one of you please shoot THOSE BASTARDS DOWN?" The jets were making one more pass; it proved to be one pass too many. The men managed to gather themselves, picked up their missile launchers and fired; the warning signal inside the cockpit of the jet started to blink, indicating a SAM (surface-to-air missile) launch. They both took evasive maneuvers; they fired their countermeasures. Then a second signal came up; both pilots were flying frantically, banking and doing barrel rolls. They had fired the last of their countermeasures; then a third signal came up. Now they were just panicking; one Stinger exploded near the jets exhaust. The jet was peppered with shrapnel; it started to smoke and then flames. The pilot ejected out just in time three seconds later; his jet exploded and went down. The second pilot of the other jet was not as fortunate. The Stinger missile exploded in just about the same spot as the other. His cockpit filled with smoke. He tried to eject, but it malfunctioned; the plane just disintegrated around him.

Now General Fawwaz was furious. His tanks and the rest of his men charged on, firing with everything they had. They were about 150 yards out when the Vulcan 134 miniguns opened fire, using armor-piercing and incendiary rounds that, with the 50-cal sniper rifles, were picking off his men like fish in a barrel. General Fawwaz's men were being cut down so fast he was sure there would be none left by the time he reached his objective. The rounds ripped through the tanks, causing some to explode. Others just started to smoke and made sharp left and right turns. This only meant that the crew was dead. The light armored troop carriers' fate was even worse than the tanks. The shells ripped through the light armor and the men inside like a rock hitting a rotten tomato. It was a gory sight; after twenty-eight tanks and 1,000 men, by the time General Fawwaz reached the rock face, he had two tanks and about two hundred men left.

The helicopters finally arrived—two and another on the way to pick up his crew. Thomas had his team take President Wilkins, Agent Adams, and the kids to the loading zone. "What are you going to do?" Willy said. "You just get everybody up there. I have a couple more things for them to deal with!" He smiled and slapped Willy on the back. "Go on, I won't be too far behind." Thomas made his way to the opening at the front of the rock face. The soldiers were about fifty yards away; he jumped in the trench where the 50-cal machine was. Surprisingly, it was not damaged by the missiles from the jets. He pulled back the bolt and let loose with deadly spray of 50-cal rounds; these too were armor-piercing rounds. He was only able to fire for about a minute when he noticed one of the tanks has its turret turning in his direction. He jumped out of the trench just in time. The 125mm round hit the trench like thunder. The concussion from the blast knocked him about twenty feet. He lay there for about ten seconds, trying to collect himself. The ringing in his ears sounded like he had his head next to a church bell; he managed to get to his feet and staggered on.

General Fawwaz and what was left of his men took great precaution as they approached the opening of the rock face. He was bound and determined to get these men. Thomas staggered and fell several times before he was able to cross the fifty yards or so to the twin 50-cal antiaircraft guns he had installed a week before. He had a makeshift seat; he got behind the gun, sat in the seat, cocked the machine gun, and waited for them. The men walked in cautiously, crouched with their guns ready to fire. Thomas spotted them coming in; he waited. There were about fifty to sixty men now walking in slowly; then he cut loose. The 50-cal rounds were kicking up all around; they were caught in the open. Some tried to dive to the ground, others tried to make a run for it. General Fawwaz was in the opening, watching the men walk in and then saw them get mowed down. Bullets were tearing his men to pieces; the rounds were tearing off big chunks of rock and kicking up dirt. After the dust had cleared, over forty men were dead or injured. His facial expression was one of disbelief. He closed the hatch of his tank, cranked it up, and started inside. The tank pulled slowly inside. Thomas had just made it to his second gun placement, another Vulcan minigun. When the tank opened fire, hitting the gun placement he just left, the ground beneath his feet shook like it was an earthquake, and the sound was so loud he thought he will never get his hearing back at this rate. He lifted the cover over the arming switch, clicked it on, and let loose once again. The rounds hit the tank, punching holes in its armor. Some of General Fawwaz's men decided to come in behind the tank. Thomas swept the gun from left to right, raking the tank and the men who foolishly came in. Body parts were blown off—legs, arms, and some were just cut in half. General Fawwaz's crew was able to get one round in the breech. Thomas saw the turret raise up; he kept firing then thought better of it and jumped out once again, just in time landing on his stomach. He still had his AR-15 that shot 50-cal rounds slung across his back; he jumped up and made his way up the path to the LZ. Several of the general's men were running at full speed, firing at the same time. Bullets ricocheted and whizzed past him. He made it to the top of the path, turned, and fired off several quick burst, emptying the thirty-round clip. He quickly reloaded; the men were making their way up the path. Now he had four frag grenades; he took two, pulled the pins, and rolled them down the path. The grenades rolled and bounced down the path. By the time the men looked up, it was too late; it was like slow motion as they exploded. Shrapnel tore through the first two men, as they were knocked off their feet, killing them. A third one was injured. Thomas pulled the pin on his last two grenades and tossed them down the path. One bounced off a rock and was about three feet off the ground when it went off, killing the wounded soldier and another. The second grenade exploded, wounding three more.

CHAPTER TWENTY-THREE

THE TWO CHOPPERS landed. President Wilkins, Agent Adams, and the kids (Megan, James, Karen, and Sandra) plus four of Thomas's team got into the first one. In the second one was the nurses and four more of Thomas's team. The helicopters began to take off. Then President Wilkins asked the pilot, "What about the other men?"

"THERE WILL BE a third chopper to pick them up." The nurses and the other men in the second chopper asked the same question of their pilot and were told the same. Thomas fired another thirty-round clip down the path. He looked up and saw the choppers lifting off. He loaded another clip and made his way over to where the rest of the team was kneeling down. "What's going on?"

"THERE IS A third chopper on the way," they said in unison.

"WHEN WILL IT be here? Because in about two minutes, we are going to have about one hundred men coming up that path anytime now!" They started to get into defensive positions. They all started to check to see how much ammo they had left. "I have four."

"SAME HERE."

"ME TOO." THOMAS looked at them and smiled, and they looked at him like he was crazy. He turned and ran toward the black tarps that Eva saw on the first night. They all got up one after another and followed. He pulled back the first tarp to reveal a DPV (desert patrol vehicle). They immediately began to pull back the other two tarps that revealed two more DPVs. There were helmets in the seats. They began to put on the helmets and jumped in the seats, started them up, and took off. A few of General Fawwaz's men made it up the path to see the DPV pulling away. They took aim and pulled the triggers. "CLICK." Their rifles misfired once again; these men had gotten away.

Thomas and Eva were in the first DPV, Willy and Steve in the second, then Oscar and Lyle in the third. They were heading for an abandoned airstrip some forty miles away. The DPVs were cruising at 45 mph. Everyone was in good spirits and glad to be out of the situation. They had just left; they would soon be out of this country and on their way back home. The third chopper was supposed to take them to this airstrip, but they didn't have time to wait. They had traveled for about fifteen minutes; just twenty minutes more and they would be out of here when explosions erupted all around them. Eva looked back to see several tanks and other vehicles. Each driver floored the DPVs. Their top speed was just a little over 60 mph. The tank commander aimed at the vehicles again and fired, once again missing them as they zigzagged to keep the tanks from getting a bead on them. This went on what seemed like eternity when you know your life is at stake, but it was just two minutes in reality. Eva kept looking back. There was nothing they could do except to try and outrun them. The next round of shells got very close. One hit very close to Steve and Willy's DPV, knocking it almost on its side. Willy managed to ride on two wheels to keep it from tipping over; it landed roughly, and he fought for control.

This was not looking good for them; they were sitting ducks out here. The tanks now had the vehicles in range and were ready to fire when hell seemed to erupt all around them. Eva grabbed Thomas's arm and shook it hard and started making gestures to look back. He managed to take a quick peek and saw the tanks exploding. "Predator One, this is Firefly."

"Go ahead."

"We are closing your back door and will meet you at the airstrip."

"Roger that." Firefly was an AC 130 gunship that was armed with 40mm cannon, 105mm cannon, and Vulcan Gatlin 30mm six-barrel minigun. The firepower that this plane possessed was incredible. Thomas felt sorry for the soldiers that were at the receiving end of this massive destruction this plane was putting on them.

The two choppers landed at the abandoned airstrip. There was one C–130 cargo plane with several armed men standing around it. Everyone was rushed from the helicopters to the plane; a medical staff was on board. The president's insistence on knowing what happened to Thomas and his men went unanswered, as men rushed around attending to their medical needs. He saw the helicopters taking off; maybe they were on their way back to pick them up. Megan and her friends were wondering also, how could they go off and leave the people that just had just saved their lives? The planes' engines roared to life, and they felt it start to move. It rumbled down the runway and then lifted off. It was a great relief to know finally they were on their way home. The pilots changed their call sign to Air Force One. The president was safe, and so were the children. They would fly to Ramstein AFB and then back to the US. Megan and her friends got the adventure but just not the way they had planned it. People had died from their stupid mistake. Her father was right. Your "decisions can affect others and just not yourself." It was a tough lesson, but it was one that would affect her for the rest of her life.

CHAPTER TWENTY-FOUR

WILLY'S DPV WAS becoming increasingly difficult to control. The right front tire was making a loud sound of metal against metal, and it started to smoke. He could hear Thomas on his earpiece telling him, "We are almost there." The three DPVs pulled up to the airstrip. They jumped out. The C-130 gunship that had just saved them was coming in to land. High fives and slaps on the backs and big grins were on their faces. The C-130 landed and opened its cargo door; they quickly got on board. There was no room for the DPVs, so they put satchel charges on them and got back on the plane. As the plane made its way down the runway, they could hear the explosions. They had to be destroyed so the enemy could not use them. Everyone was happy to be finally leaving the country. A great relief could be seen on all of their faces. This was Eva's first mission; she was glad that she survived and understood why the men could get hooked on doing this. It was such an adrenaline rush, but she's not sure if she would do this again. They were just five minutes into their flight when Thomas was called to the cockpit. "What is it?" The pilot pointed to the instrument panel; a small blip was on the screen and moving fast. "Great." A fighter jet was closing in on them fast. Then a second blip then a third. It had fired missiles. The pilot quickly engaged their Angel fire countermeasure; the reason it was called this was because the flares came from underneath its wings. It was quite impressive; it looked just like an angel's wing. It was so bright that it lit up the night sky. The C-130 banked hard right as the missiles exploded behind them. Thomas told the pilot to open the cargo door. He quickly made his way back to where everyone was sitting; he walked past only saying, "Willy, strap up."

Eva was looking confused and scared. "What is going on?" No one said a word except for Thomas and Willy who were talking to each other. They both had picked up two portable Stinger missiles, took aim, and fired. The pilot in the fighter jet was surprised to see a warning signal on his instrument panel, but he knew what it was. He banked hard left then right and released his countermeasures. One missile exploded, but one remained chasing him through sky. He tried a steep climb and then a quick dive. The missile was hunting him down and getting closer; he banked right and then hard left. He was not going to get away; the second stinger exploded about twenty feet from his jet engine. The plane shook and lights and alarms were going off in his cockpit; he had to eject. Willy and Thomas were watching from the cargo hold on the C-130, and they saw the explosion. All Thomas was hoping for was that the pilot would just turn and leave. He never thought they would actually hit the jet. He told the pilot to close the cargo door. He looked at Willy and laughed. "You know that should not have worked." Willy answered back, "You're right, but I'm sure glad it did." They could relax now; it was finally over. They both sat down and began taking off their gear, and everyone followed suit. They had to refuel in midair before they made their way back to Germany. The pilots of their plane had contacted the other plane with the president and the kids on it. The president heard the news that Thomas and the rest of his team had made it out, and everyone cheered. It was quite a moment; it was one that you just had to be there to appreciate it. The planes were just a few minutes apart but were landing at two separate airfields. Another mission accomplished. This was to be the last go-around for Thomas. Being in his early forties, it was time to call it quits. The rest of the team had been thinking the same. They had overcome some incredible odds on several of their missions, but this one they knew it was nothing but God that got them through. And there was no need to push your luck; it was time to call it quits.

THE END